# Périgord Prehistory

BRIGITTE AND GILLES DELLUC
ALAIN ROUSSOT
JULIA ROUSSOT-LARROQUE

Translated by Angela Caldwell and Stanley L. Olivier

ÉDITIONS SUD OUEST

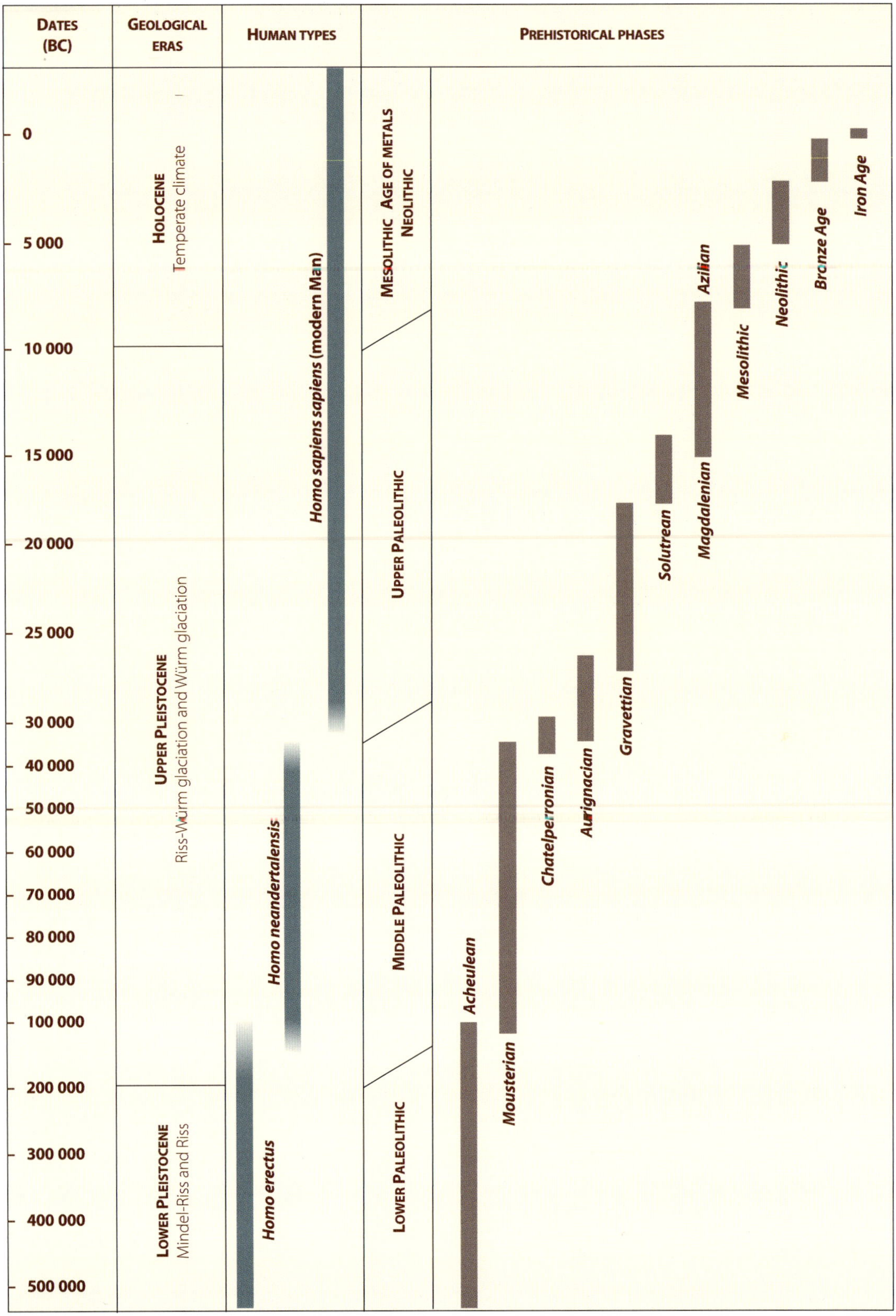
DATES (BC)
GEOLOGICAL ERAS
HUMAN TYPES
PREHISTORICAL PHASES
0
5 000
10 000
15 000
20 000
25 000
30 000
40 000
50 000
60 000
70 000
80 000
90 000
100 000
200 000
300 000
400 000
500 000
HOLOCENE
Temperate climate
UPPER PLEISTOCENE
Riss-Würm glaciation and Würm glaciation
LOWER PLEISTOCENE
Mindel-Riss and Riss
Homo sapiens sapiens (modern Man)
Homo neandertalensis
Homo erectus
MESOLITHIC
AGE OF METALS
NEOLITHIC
UPPER PALEOLITHIC
MIDDLE PALEOLITHIC
LOWER PALEOLITHIC
Acheulean
Mousterian
Chatelperronian
Aurignacian
Gravettian
Solutrean
Magdalenian
Azilian
Mesolithic
Neolithic
Bronze Age
Iron Age

# Exploring Prehistory in Périgord

*Wherever humans have lived, they have left bones, tools and weapons made of stone, animal bone or metal, a few grams of charcoal, small pebbles and virtually invisible grains of plant pollen. However, these odds and ends would be of little importance if we could not breathe life back into them.*

This is the work of the prehistorian (or protohistorian for periods closer to recorded history). *To understand human history, you have to be able to distinguish between Christopher Columbus and Karl Marx, between Gutenberg and Napoleon Bonaparte. To understand prehistory and protohistory, you have to show a great deal of patience, advancing one step at a time along the paths of knowledge. Otherwise, it would be too easy to get lost.*

*It is, then, a succession of periods in prehistory that we invite you to explore with us, without travelling too far from Périgord since, with the exception of our oldest ancestors, people from every period of prehistory have lived here in turn.*

# The dawn of time

A few dizzying facts and figures:

- The Earth was formed 4 billion years ago.
- Life (in the form of small blue algae) appeared 2 billion years ago.
- Dinosaurs walked the Earth 200 million years ago.
- The first man appeared 2.5 million years ago in Africa.
- Humans have only been living in Périgord for 450,000 years.
- The most distant ancestors of modern man, *Homo sapiens*, appeared 200,000 years ago in Africa.
- *Homo sapiens* arrived in France only 35,000 years ago. This was Cro-Magnon man, responsible for the cave paintings in Lascaux 17,000 to 18,000 years ago. Quite recently, in fact.

## Dividing up prehistoric periods

Geological periods are divided into eras – primary, secondary, tertiary and quaternary. One of the main features of the end of the tertiary era and the entire quaternary era is the presence of Man. Three major periods succeeded each other during the Quaternary era – the Palaeolithic (Lower, Middle and Upper) or Carved Stone Age, the Neolithic or Polished Stone Age and the ages of metals. Each of these major periods is divided into a number of ages, usually reflecting the appearance of the implements made by Man. Each age took its name from a major site in which extensive traces of the period have been found. The site is then described as "eponymous" - Aurignac and the Aurignacian Period, La Gravette and the Gravettian Period, Le Moustier and the Mousterian Period etc.

## Setting the date!

Chronology is calculated using a range of physical and chemical methods such as Carbon 14 dating for items no more than 40,000 years old. The dates are indicated either as B.P. (before present), fixed by convention as 1950 A.D., or B.C. (before Christ). For the Palaeolithic Era, dates are generally given as B.P. whe-

**The calendars of the Palaeolithic Era**
Father Henri Breuil was photographed by his assistant, Father André Glory, in Laussel *circa* 1954. He was at the pinnacle of his career, a member of the Institute and referred to as the "Pope of Prehistory". He is thought to have made his first visit to Laussel on 15th April 1908, as part of the committee that came to decide whether or not the Solutrean was more recent than the Aurignacian. The committee carried out the same task, on the same day, in Le Ruth. Father Breuil is also famous for having defined the six subdivisions of the Magdalenian Era ■

reas dates within the protohistoric period tend to follow the calendar i.e. B.P. or B.C. Dates obtained using the Carbon 14 dating method are slightly more recent than the ones obtained using other methods and may sometimes be subject to correction.

**The famous "hut" in La Mouthe (Les Eyzies)**
This painted and engraved outline, whose meaning is still unknown despite its name, is among the cave art in La Mouthe. When it was discovered in 1895, the entrance to the decorated gallery was completely blocked by archaeological deposits left by several encampments during the Early Palaeolithic Era. This means that the drawings are older than the upper layers of deposits ■

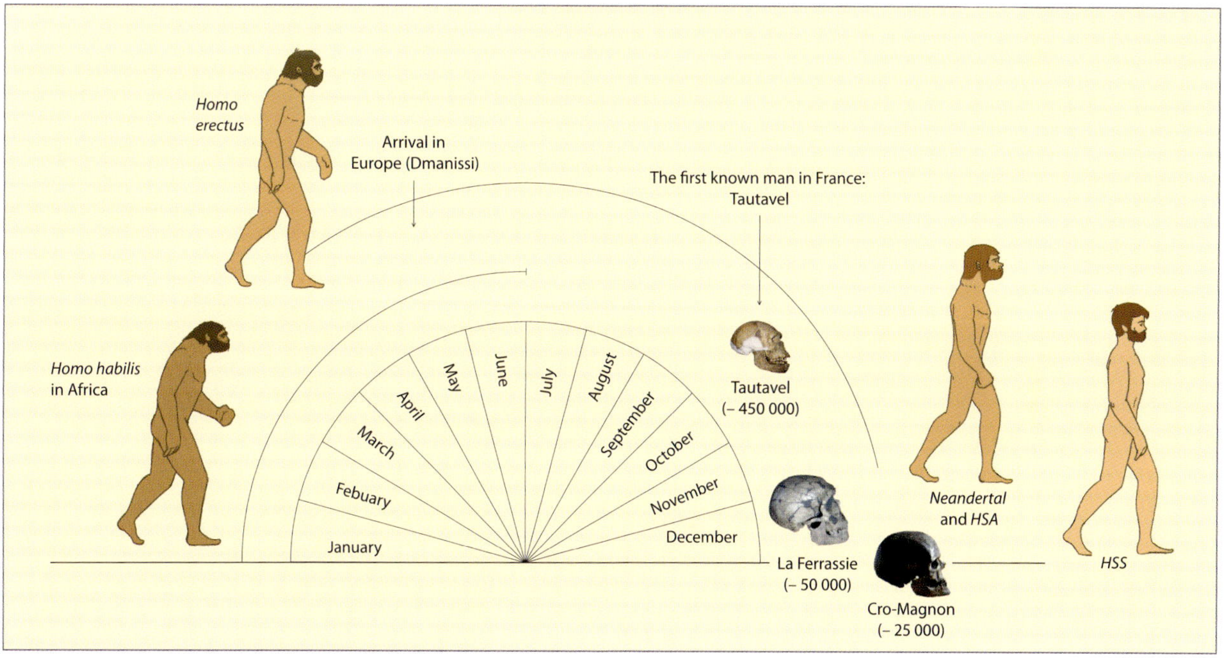


**2.5 million years of human evolution compared to a reference year**
Let's start on 1st January. The reference year begins with the first hominid, *Homo habilis*, who remained in Africa until the end of June. *Homo erectus* was born in the middle of April, also in Africa. These men reached the gateways to Europe and Asia early in May. One of them, the pre-Neanderthal *Homo erectus* from Tautavel in the Pyrénées-Orientales who is the first known man in France, lived at the end of October. The first inhabitants in Périgord were *Homo erectus*. These people are known to have lived at this period although no traces of their skeletons have been found. All that has been uncovered are traces of their encampments and tools. In mid-December, *Homo erectus* dies out, replaced by Neanderthal Man and the oldest *Homo sapiens*. The first examples of modern man, our direct ancestors, do not reach France until Christmas Day. They are *Homo sapiens sapiens,* or Cro-Magnon Man as they are usually called. Périgord has a large number of traces of Neanderthal and Cro-Magnon Man – skeletons, encampments, tools and works of art. Using our scale, History, which came into being with the invention of writing, began on New Year's Eve, 31st December, in the late morning ■

# Successive prototypes

*Men and apes have a common ancestor. Man developed from a slow evolutionary process which became individualised some 7 to 8 million years ago. This was when some distant ancestors appeared, in Africa.*

The Hominids of the Tertiary Era were small with poorly developed brains but the ability to walk upright. They were followed by Australopithecus from South and East Africa. One of them, who is 3.5 million years old, has become quite a celebrity. Her name is Lucy and she was named after one of the Beatles' songs.

### Homo habilis

The first human was *Homo habilis*, or "skilful man". He produced stone tools and lived by hunting small easily captured animals (lizards, small birds) and gathering berries etc. He made a few stone tools that were used to cut, scrape, hammer and dig. This "skilful man" was small in stature (under 1.50 metres) with a fairly small brain (650 cubic centimetres, only half as large as ours) but his morphology proves that he walked upright and his teeth resemble ours more than they do those of apes. He had no forehead but possessed a heavy brow ridge and his jaw was strong. He had no chin. *Homo habilis'* language is believed to have been very basic and his skin colour is, of course, unknown. This group of hominids appeared in Eastern and Southern Africa 2.5 million years ago and they are known to have stayed there for some one million years.

### Homo erectus

These hominids succeeded *Habilis* almost 2 million years ago in Africa and spread into Europe and Asia. *Homo erectus* was slightly taller than his ancestors. His skull retained more or less the same primitive characteristics but his brain was larger (1,000 to 1,200 cubic centimetres, two-thirds the size of ours). Endocasts taken of the inside of skulls show that these humans had an articulate language. The oldest skeleton found in France was a *Homo erectus* who lived in the Arago cave in Tautavel at the eastern end of the Pyrenees. These humans discovered the use of fire some 400,000 years ago. They lived in huts made of branches, as they did in Terra Amata, near the port of Nice. Apart from flints, their tools consisted of little more than a single tool but it is very ingenious. It is a biface, or hand ax, a more or less flat, oval or almond-shaped piece of flint. It was used for hitting, cutting and spiking. In fact, it was an all-purpose tool. Like *Habilis* before him, *Erectus* was also a hunter. Over this long period, the climate consisted of alternating cycles of cold and hot weather. The last examples of *Homo erectus* lived in La Micoque at Les Eyzies. They were the first people to live in Périgord, almost half-a-million years ago, but no skeletons have yet been uncovered. They lived here in the Lower Palaeolithic Era.

### Neanderthal Man (*Homo neanderthalensis*)

The descendents of *Erectus* were somewhat rustic but very strong individuals. At 1.60 metres, they were slightly taller with a very large brain (1,500 and even 1,600 cubic centimetres instead of 1,000), a well-developed occiput, a sloping forehead, prominent brows but no chin. These were the Neanderthals who lived in Périgord between 100,000 years and 30,000 years B.P. They were by no means brutes. In fact, they perfected their stone tools, showed a liking for colour and collections, and buried their dead in rock shelters like the one in La Ferrassie or in caves like the one at La Chapelle-aux-Saints in Corrèze. They lived in the Middle Palaeolithic Era.

## *Homo sapiens*

The last and most recent in this lineage was *Homo sapiens*, also known as Cro-Magnon Man, who appeared here some 30,000 to 35,000 years ago. Cro-Magnons were every bit as human as we are, no more attractive or intelligent than we are today. Of course, they were hunter-gatherers and they did not have our cultural knowledge but they were able to produce a range of tools using blades fashioned from large pieces of flint, make objects out of bone or deer antlers, and create weapons for hunting. They learned to sew. They made jewellery and bric-a-brac. They invented drawing, engraving and painting on rocks and on cave walls. They sculpted and modelled small statuettes. Theirs was the Upper Palaeolithic Era.

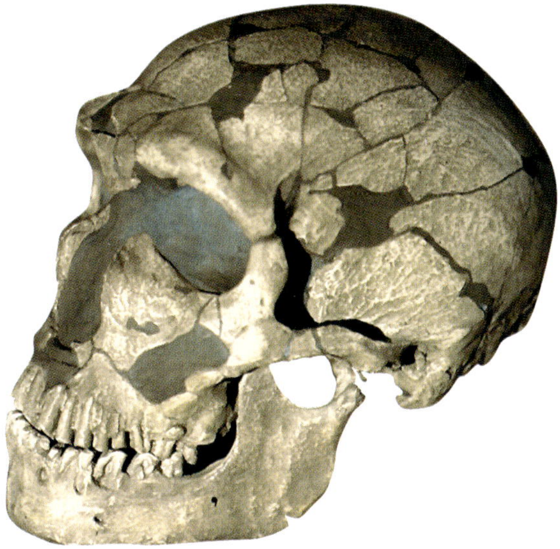

**Neanderthal Man**
This is not the skull of one of our direct ancestors; it is the skull of a Neanderthal man. He lived in the Les Eyzies area some 40,000 years ago. The skull was discovered in La Ferrassie, with a dozen others of adults and children. The Neanderthals are descendents of the *Homo erectus* who came from Africa some one million years ago. Approximately 30,000 years ago, they coexisted with *Homo sapiens* – 1% to 4% of the genetic makeup of European and Asian *Homo sapiens* comes from Neanderthal Man ■

**Cro-Magnon Man**
This skull belongs to the most famous of our direct ancestors and it is approximately 27,000 years old. This *Homo sapiens* is one of the five people discovered in 1868 in the small Cro-Magnon rock shelter in Les Eyzies. Called "the Old Man", he was probably no more than 50 years old but that was a good age in those days. This type of human, who resembles us, did not appear first in the Les Eyzies region. He is known to have had ancestors in the Near East 100,000 years ago and even in Ethiopia 200,000 years ago ■

# Prehistoric Man's environment

*Over these hundreds of thousands of years, the climate varied. There were at least four long periods of extreme cold known as ice ages, separated by periods of warming, the interglacial periods.*

## Hot and cold

The last two ice ages are named after the Riss (300,000 to 125,000 B.P.) and Würm (115,000 to 10,000 B.P), two tributaries of the Danube in which the glaciers of the river basin were studied.

During the last of the ice ages, the climate was much colder than it is today (5 °C cooler, on average), reminiscent of present-day Scandinavia with typical periglacial flora and fauna in tundra dotted with more or less dense tree growth. During these cold spells, however, the climate varied depending on altitude and latitude, proximity to the sea or mountains and also the years and centuries. A small rise in temperature produced a marshland forest of alders, birch and pines, a taiga. A few more degrees and the climate resembled our own, not unlike the interstadial of Lascaux, 17,000 to 18,000 years ago. The flora and fauna changed accordingly.

Neanderthals and Cro-Magnons lived through the Würm glaciation but it would be a mistake to imagine them living on pack ice among polar bears, suffering through blizzards and long polar nights. They were not Inuits.

**Reindeer migrations**
Some 20,000 to 25,000 years ago, Les Eyzies underwent a period of intense cold, the last Ice Age. Reindeer were well adapted to the cold and they would migrate over huge distances depending on the season. These were the days of mammoths, woolly rhinoceros and musk oxen. They were actively hunted because reindeer filled the larders, toolboxes and jewellery boxes of Cro-Magnons (drawing by Eric Guerrier, Le Pataud rock shelter Museum). Man, though, did not feed solely on reindeer. Humans were omnivorous ■

It is the study of animal bones (large herbivores, small mammals and birds), plant pollens, wood and mineral sediment that allows us to reconstruct the climate.

## Countless caves

There are numerous caves in the limestone areas of Périgord. The rock contains natural fissures in the form of diaclases (vertical cracks) or stratification joints (horizontal cracks) that have been widened by underground streams which gouge out galleries, some wide, some narrow. These passages were later partially filled in with clay soil and calcite concretions (stalactites, stalagmites, flows etc.).

Man used cave mouths as homes, or as the last resting-place of the deceased. Cro-Magnons, especially from the Lascaux period onwards (17,000 or 18,000 years ago), pushed deep into the galleries and passageways where, by the flickering light of tallow lamps, they painted the walls. These decorated caves were places of worship, underground sanctuaries. Some of the caves, like the one in Saint-Cirq, are fairly close to the surface but most of them are deep underground and sometimes difficult to access e.g. Font-de-Gaume, Lascaux, les Combarelles, Bernifal, Bara-Bahau and Villars in Dordogne; Pech-Merle and Cougnac in Lot; Chauvet in Ardèche; Niaux in Ariège and Altamira in Spain.

A few of them are vast, running over a distance of several miles. One such is the cave in Rouffignac which visitors tour on board a small electric train.

## Homes for prehistoric hunter-gatherers

Very early in human development, Man built houses – huts with frames made from branches (or even from the tusks of mammoths in the great plains of Russia) covered with hides and carpeted with furs. These homes were either erected in the open, or beneath the overhang of a cliff forming a rock-shelter, or at the mouth of a cave.

OPPOSITE PAGE
**Cold and heat**
The ice of a very cold winter turns the natural environment white at the foot of a cliff in Les Eyzies while, in the foreground, the heat of the sun reveals recent work in the field. The same image, in fact, reflects the chill temperatures of the Reindeer Age and the transition into the milder temperate days of the Farming Age. During the Würm glaciation, the mean temperature was 5°C lower than it is today. The climate was harsh but not polar ■

Cro-Magnon Man sometimes had huts in the open with paved flooring, as was the case in the Lower Isle Valley. Contrary to legend, these people never actually lived in dark, damp caves which would quickly fill with smoke. They did, however, venture inside, sometimes over a considerable distance, to paint and engrave pictures on the cave walls.

At that time, Man was a hunter-gatherer and fisherman, living off the land without farming or breeding livestock. People led a semi-nomadic life, settling briefly in one area then moving on in search of game, following the migration of reindeer and the course of salmon swimming up rivers.

For 100,000 years, they buried some of their dead, sometimes in rock shelters near their homes.

## A WIDE RANGE OF ANIMALS

- Like plants, wildlife also varies with the climate. During very cold periods, musk oxen, mammoths and woolly rhinoceros, reindeer, wolves and certain small animals (such as lemmings, hares and polar foxes, ptarmigan and snowy owls) all thrive in a landscape filled with typical flora. Forests, especially deciduous woodland, recede, leaving only mosses and lichens during the very coldest periods, with a few copses of willows and dwarf birch.
- When the climate warms slightly, elk, bison, reindeer, mammoths and woolly rhinoceros graze beneath the trees while huge herds of reindeer, horses and aurochs roam the wide open spaces during massive, regular periods of migration. Ibexes and chamois leap from rock to boulder, having not yet sought refuge in the high mountain ranges. Felines hunt mainly at night and bears retire to caves to hibernate, drop their cubs or die. During the Mousterian Era, there were cave bears; in the days of Cro-Magnon man, there were brown bears.
- What happened when the climate heated up a little more? Temperate forest appeared, with oaks, hazels, Norway pines, juniper and sometimes even walnut trees. Between the woodland were meadows full of hares, aurochs, stags and hinds, roe deer, wild boar and the species of small animals (birds and small mammals) that we still see around us today.

### The first farmers

Their successors some 12,000 years B.C. lived in a milder climate and huge herds of reindeer headed northwards again. During the Neolithic and metal Ages, Man liked to settle in rock shelters, at cave mouths or in the open air. They buried their dead beneath dolmens then in burial caves. Since crop and animal farming, metalworking and ceramics aroused a degree of envy, they made weapons to defend themsevles against other men, and built the first fortifications. By convention, Julius Caesar's conquest of Gaul in 52 B.C. marks the end of the prehistoric period and the beginning of the great history of France and its people.

OPPOSITE
**Chamber of Paintings Villars Cave**
Dordogne has thousands of caves and several dozen of them were decorated during the Palaeolithic Era. Sometimes, they are difficult to access. Lascaux is superb, with its walls coated in an immaculate veil of calcite, and it was undoubtedly selected as the site of an exceptional sanctuary. Palaeolithic Man, though, did not live in dark, humid caves that would quickly fill with smoke ■

# Dates and people

*Prehistory proceeded by trial and error for nearly two centuries before becoming recognized as a true science. Today, it is taught in our universities. Several dates will illustrate the principal steps along the path to progress from the early 19th century, a time when the very ancient history of humankind had not yet been recognized.*

**A historic excursion**
When Edouard Lartet and Henry Christy arrived in Les Eyzies in August 1863, they headed straight for this small opening known as the Richard Cave. It was there that a fragment of an archaeological layer had been found. Its inclusion in an exhibition in Paris in 1862 had encouraged them to make the trip. Located in the cliff overlooking the Beune Valley, this small cave in Les Eyzies was lived in for a short period during the Solutrean but was a more important settlement in the Upper Magdalenian ■

## The precursors

**1810-1816.** A professor and occasional letter-press printer, François Jouannet, explored Écornebœuf, which overlooks the town of Périgueux and the ancient "city" of Vésone. There he found flint arrowheads, and flaked polished axes which were attributed to the Ancient Gauls at that time. He then explored the Pech de l'Aze cave near Sarlat and Combe Grenal cave near Domme, finding large quantites of worked flints and animal bones.
**1834.** Discussing the Badegoule cave near Le Lardin, Jouannet suggested the existence of a Worked Stone Age that predated the Polished Stone and Bronze Ages.

**A fossilised floor.** Hardened by infiltrations of water with a high lime content, the archaeological layer in the Richard Cave could be cut into blocks and slabs. Lartet and Christy sent samples to several museums. This "breach" in the Richard Cave contained flints worked by humans, pebbles, the bones of animals that the inhabitants had hunted and eaten (mainly reindeer) and, sometimes, by chance, small stone or bone artefacts decorated with engravings (Périgueux Museum) ■

**1847-1860.** The publication of *Les Antiquités celtiques et antédiluviennes,* ("Celtic and Antediluvian Antiquites") by Jacques Boucher de Perthes marked the official coming-of-age of Prehistory thanks to the geological, palaeontological and archaeological discoveries made in the Abbeville region in Somme.
**1863-1864.** Édouard Lartet, a magistrate in South-Western France, and English industrialist Henry Christy, Lartet's friend and patron, arrived in Les Eyzies in August 1863. For several months, they walked along the banks of the Vézère and explored some of the most prestigious sites: the Richard cave in Les Eyzies, Gorge d'Enfer (one of its rock shelters now bears Lartet's name), Laugerie-Basse, Laugerie-Haute, La Madeleine, Le Moustier etc. This period saw the beginning of intensive digs in the region.
**1868.** Several human skeletons were found during roadworks, with a number of Aurignacian flints, at a small Cro-Magnon rock shelter in Les Eyzies, near the railway station. In 1874, Armand de Quatrefages and Ernest-Théodore Hamy used these skeletons to define a new fossil race – Cro-Magnon man.

**1874.** Founding of the *Société historique et archéologique du Périgord* (Périgord historical and archaeological society). It has published countless works on the region's prehistory right up to the present day.
**1888.** Maurice Féaux and Michel Hardy dug up a Magdalenian skeleton just outside the small Raymonden cave near Chancelade. Numerous mobile works of art were also discovered there.

The days of Peyrony and Breuil

During the second half of the 19th century, several archaeologists excavated known sites and discovered still others. Gradually, a more exact chronology of prehistoric periods was developed (by E. Lartet, Gabriel de Mortillet, and Edouard Piette). However, the research was often too hasty and poorly-organised; many sites were damaged for ever. It was not until the 20th century that digs were properly conducted, notably by Denis Peyrony. It was also at this time that Palaeolithic cave art became known and acknowledged, thanks to the work and writings of Father Henri Breuil.
**1895.** Engravings and paintings were discovered in La Mouthe cave in Les Eyzies. It was the first decorated cave discovered in the Périgord, and the third in Europe as a whole, after Altamira in Spain and the Chabot cave in Gard.
**1901.** On 8th September, Louis Capitan, Henri Breuil and Denis Peyrony were exploring the cave at Les Combarelles when they found some engravings on the walls. Four days later, D. Peyrony found paintings and engravings in Font-de-Gaume. Following on from the discoveries made at La Mouthe, these two significant finds contributed to the official recognition of the age of cave art which, until then, had been contested by certain archaeologists. In the following year, D. Peyrony discovered the Bernifal cave and its engravings.

**Two great names**
Teacher Denis Peyrony (centre) and Father Henri Breuil (right) were the two great names in Prehistory in the Vézère area in the early 20th century. They it was who undertook meticulous studies of large sites and the great decorated caves. Here, on 15th April 1908, they can be seen in Le Ruth near Le Moustier in the company of E. Cartailhac (left). They have just checked that the Aurignacian Era preceded the Solutrean, a fact that had previously been contested by Gabriel de Mortillet, author of the first chronology of prehistoric times. This marked a victory in the "Battle of the Aurignacian" ■

**A few years before the Great War**
In 1908, a learned doctor from Bordeaux named G. Lalanne had his workmen conduct a huge dig under the Laussel rock shelter 6 kilometres from Les Eyzies, in the Beune Valley. This view of the archaeological dig, taken *circa* 1911-1912, speaks volumes. However, other archaeologists, notably D. Peyrony, conducted more scrupulous and more meticulous digs at that time ■

**1908.** A Swiss archaeologist, Otto Hauser, who was making money from the sites in Périgord, uncovered a Neanderthal skeleton in Le Moustier and immediately sold it to the Berlin Museum.
**1909.** D. Peyrony, who had been exploring La Ferrassie since 1902, found the first of many Mousterian human burials. Significant deposits dating from the Upper Palaeolithic era would continue to be uncovered there until 1921.

**La Mouthe: the bison**
This engraving of a bison was the first such decoration noticed on 11th April 1895 by G. Berthoumeyrou after the entrance to the gallery had been cleared. It is located more than 100 metres from the mouth on the wall of a small chamber, and is surrounded by 9 other bison, 2 mountain goats and a stag, as well as various other markings. The style of the figures dates them from the Early Magdalenian; they still have some archaic features. The horns are shown almost from the front and it is clear that the horns of prehistoric bison were much longer than those of their modern counterparts. The cave contains countless other engravings ■

**1909.** The excavation at the Cap Blanc rock shelter in Marquay revealed an animal frieze carved on the walls. It was the first time carvings had been found in a cave.
**1910-1913.** D. Peyrony undertook a state-funded dig in La Madeleine.
**1911-1912.** Bas-reliefs of human beings were discovered in the Laussel rock shelter. A carving of a fish was observed on the roof of a rock shelter at Gorge d'Enfer in Les Eyzies.
**1913.** 31st December. A law was passed to protect historic monuments, including all present and future prehistoric sites. The same year, at Peyrony's suggestion, the government bought the ruins of the Château des Eyzies for use as a museum. The first exhibition opened in 1918, and the museum was officially inaugurated in 1923.
**1921-1935.** D. Peyrony conducted a dig at Laugerie-Haute. This major site enabled the experts to establish an exact chronology for several phases in the Upper Palaeolithic Era.
**1931 and 1933.** Twenty-seven bronze axes were discovered nearby. They were listed in 1943.

## Modern times

Digs became more precise and the increased popularity of archaeology led to the discovery of some superb decorated caves.
**1940.** Discovery of the Lascaux cave by Marcel Ravidat and his three friends. The cave was immediately authenticated by Father Breuil. Extensive work on the interior allowed the cave to be opened to the public in 1948.
**1941.** 27th September. A law was passed to regulate archaeological digs, during the time of the Vichy government. It was not validated until 1945. After that, digs required authorisation from the State.
**1952-1963.** Father André Glory traced the 1,500 engravings in Lascaux and carried out digs in the Well in 1960-1961.
**1952.** Publication of Father Breuil's *Quatre cents siècles d'art pariétal* (Four hundred centuries of cave art).
**1952.** Discovery of prehistoric engravings in the cave in Saint-Cirq.
**1953-1964.** Hallam L. Movius explored a major Aurignacian and Gravettian site in Pataud and it became the benchmark for this period. The dig was taken up again in 2005 by Laurent Chiotti and Roland Nespoulet (from the *Muséum national d'histoire naturelle*).
**1953-1965.** François Bordes conducted a dig at Combe Grenal, a major Acheulean and Mousterian site.
**1956.** Led by Charles Plassard, Louis-René Nougier and Romain Robert, archaeologists discovered prehistoric drawings in the Rouffignac cave which had first been reported by 1948 by the Spéléo-Club de Périgueux (pot-holing club).
**1958.** Prehistoric paintings were found in the Villars cave by the Spéléo-Club de Périgueux and A. Glory.

**Speleologists.** At the end of the Second World War, potholing became increasingly popular, leading to the discovery of numerous decorated caves. The Spéléo-Club de Périgueux notified the authorities of drawings in the cave in Rouffignac, in particular the Rhinoceros Frieze which it photographed in 1948 when camping in the cave. The prehistorian responsible for the cave said the paintings had been done by members of the French Resistance Movement. They were not officially recognised as the work of prehistoric artists until 1956

**Modern digs in the Pataud cave.** From 1953 to 1964, an American team under Hallam Movius, Professor at the University of Harvard, conducted some methodical digs in one of the few intact sites in Les Eyzies. From the explored section of this major site, he dug up two million objects (human and animal bones, flint and bone tools, knapping waste, objets d'art and jewellery etc.). Pollens and charcoal enabled him to date some forty successive periods of occupation and specify the corresponding climatic conditions

**1959.** Henri Delporte conducted a dig at the Facteur rock shelter and uncovered a female statuette dating from the Gravettian.
**1963.** Lascaux cave was closed to the public after natural changes to the interior threatened the existence of the paintings.
**1965.** Publication of *Préhistoire de l'art occidental* (Prehistory of Western Art) by André Leroi-Gourhan.
**1967.** F. Bordes conducted a dig at Le Pech de l'Aze (where he had first worked in 1948).
**1969-1981.** Jean-Philippe Rigaud conducted a dig at the Vaufrey cave near Domme.
**1984.** Publication of F. Bordes' *Leçons sur le Paléolithique* (Lessons on the Palaeolithic).
**2000.** The Cussac cave was discovered by speleologist, Marc Delluc.
These are the main dates that have marked the history of research in Périgord. To them should be added many other discoveries of cave art, methodic studies of decorated caves (by Claude Barrière, Brigitte et Gilles Delluc, Alain Roussot), and new digs or the relaunch of earlier digs such as the one at La Ferrassie by H. Delporte (1968-1973), Le Flageolet by J.-Ph. Rigaud (1960-1984) and the Castanet rock shelter by Randall White since 1994 etc.

**A new decorated cave in Upper Périgord**
Having observed a column of steam rising from rock, the members of the Spéléo-Club de Périgueux uncovered the entrance to the vast, superb Villars Cave in 1953. In 1958, they discovered the drawings decorating the walls. The cave soon attracted the attention of prehistorians H. Breuil, A. Glory, F. Bordes and (here) A. Leroi-Gourhan

# The Early Palaeolithic

*It is difficult to specify when the first humans settled in Périgord. The discovery of primitive-looking tools in very old alluvial deposits has occurred here and there by chance, especially in the Isle valley.*

**The all-purpose tool**
A biface is a block of flint, or sometimes a pebble or a large piece of stone, retouched on both sides. Its tip is more or less pointed and the opposite end, the heel, is more or less rounded. The earliest bifaces were used in Africa in very ancient periods. In Europe, they are typical of the Early Palaeolithic and Mousterian and their shapes vary from one era to another. They also differ in size and may have been used to break bones, cut branches or perhaps scrape skins. They had no handles ■

It was not until the third period of glaciation – called Riss – that real settlement sites existed in this region, at Pech de l'Aze, La Micoque, and at Grotte Vaufrey where lower strata date to 450,000 years ago. These layers contain industries characterized by bifaces – stone tools worked on both faces – and tools made using retouched flakes such as points, scrapers, notched tools, backed knives, etc. These industries bear the name Acheulean (from Saint-Acheul on the outskirts of Amiens in the Somme valley where they were first defined in 1872).

Several varieties of Acheulean industries are defined on the basis of distinctive shapes of bifaces, the presence or proportions of certain tools, and the knapping technique used. Acheulean variants include Southern Acheulean, Clactonian (as defined in Clacton-on-Sea in England), which is equivalent to the Tayacian described by Peyrony at La Micoque, Micoquian (which is an offshoot of Final Acheulean also found at La Micoque), and others.

The controlled use of fire dates from the Acheulean period. We know this because of the many organised, structured fire pits discovered by F. Bordes at Le Pech de l'Aze.

In Périgord, no human remains have been recovered from this period. There were not yet any organised grave sites. However, the Tautavel cave in Pyrénées-Orientales, has yielded numerous human bones, including a large number of skulls mixed with worked tools and animal bones. These were the bones of pre-Neanderthal *Homo erectus*.

Man had already acquired a taste for the beautiful by the Acheulean period. Some of the bifaces show high-quality craftsmanship and regularity in form, suggesting that the craftsman went beyond the need to merely create an efficient tool.

This period ended some 100,000 years ago.

## ☛ LA MICOQUE

This famous site, which opens in a south-westerly direction, is located on the right bank of a stream called the Manaurie, 500 metres above its confluence with the Vézère, just upriver from Laugerie-Haute. It is not a rock-shelter, but rather an open-air site at the base of a small limestone cliff about fifteen metres above the present course of the stream and its bank of river pebbles.

Discovered in 1895 by E. Rivière, the site was excavated indiscriminately by several archaeologists, then intensively by O. Hauser between 1906 and 1914. He it was who coined the name "Micoquian" in 1916 to describe an industry peculiar to this site. This term was used again by H. Breuil, following digs by D. Peyrony between 1929 and 1932, after the site had been purchased by the State.

In 1956, Bordes conducted a test dig at La Micoque. In 1969, H. Laville and Jean-Philippe Rigaud completed a detailed stratigraphic study, and in 1983 a multi-disciplinary team of researchers conducted an in-depth study of the site.

The stratigraphic data from La Micoque is important, since the six successive Acheulian occupations there correspond to the Riss and Early Würm glaciations.

The top layer of the site contains Micoquian industries (Final Acheulean) characterized by elongated bifaces with wide bases, fine points, and slightly concave edges. Recent digs have not found any more Micoquian items.

❒ The exterior of the site is open to the public. For a guided tour, book at the visitors centre in Font-de-Gaume: Tel. +33 (0) 553 068 600; email: fontdegaume@monuments-nationaux.fr

**A very old settlement in La Micoque**

For more than 200,000 years, various Acheulian groups lived on the banks of the Manaurie stream a short distance from the Vézère, at the foot and in front of a small rocky escarpment. The archaeological layers are superimposed to a depth of almost 10 metres and the last one, from the Late Acheulian, contained elongated bifaces with finely-retouched tips and slightly concave edges. They were referred to as "Micoquian bifaces" ■

## ☛ LE PECH DE L'AZE

Between Sarlat and Carsac, a road and a disused railroad track follow the small Font de Farge valley. There are four prehistoric sites at the foot of a limestone outcrop that crowns Pech de l'Aze hill (it means "Donkey Hill" in the local vernacular).

Pech I and II are located at the two extremities of a 70-metre cave which passes through a limestone outcrop. The first entrance is of historic importance because it was probably the first prehistoric site to be explored in Périgord (by Jouannet in 1815). In the 1818 issue of the *Calendrier du département de La Dordogne*, he expressed his amazement at the bones that had accumulated in the cave together with small fragments of black flint.

Later, a number of archaeologists visited the cave including Lartet and Christy in 1863. More recent digs were undertaken by Peyro-

*(Contd. on p. 19)*

# The Middle Palaeolithic

*At the end of the Riss glaciation, industries diversified and pointed the way to the Mousterian period.*

**Typical tools**
Bifaces, points and scrapers are the three "benchmark fossils" of the Mousterian but some sixty other types of tools have been described. In addition to flint, hyaline quartz (rock crystal) was sometimes worked, as it was here in Laussel. At the bottom right is a Levallois core (Aquitaine Museum, Bordeaux) ■

The Mousterian, the days of Neanderthal Man, developed during the Riss-Würm interglacial period and Early Würm glaciation, some 115,000 to 35,000 years ago. It was discovered in 1863-64 by Lartet and Christy at Le Moustier. In 1869, G. de Mortillet proposed to name comparable industries "Moustier Types" and in 1872 he called the corresponding period the "Mousterian".

The Moustier site was explored more thoroughly in the early 20th century by Peyrony, and its industries were studied more closely around 1950 by François Bordes and Maurice Bourgon. The Mousterian consists of a complex industrial period with several distinct aspects distinguished by their technology and typology. Bordes defined five major groups.

Cordiform or triangular bifaces were still present in some places (Mousterian of Acheulean tradition). A range of tools was made from flakes including more than sixty, well-defined, more developed types. Points and above all scrapers were the most characteristic.

A means of knapping known as the Levallois technique was developed in the Acheulean. This procedure consisted of shaping a block of raw material (a core), such that a flake of predetermined shape could be detached, then possibly altered to make a tool.

Neanderthal Man occupied much of Périgord at that time, often living outdoors on the

ny in 1908, by René Vaufrey in 1929, and by François Bordes and M. Bourgon in 1948 and 1951. The latter two discovered the second entrance to the cave or Pech II. From then on, Bordes dedicated several years to the dig in Pech de l'Aze, exploring a small nearby cave (Pech III), and discovering a vast collapsed rock-shelter, Pech IV, 100 metres downstream (the dig has been directed by Harold Dibble since 2000).

The entire complex made a major contribution to a deeper understanding of the Lower and Middle Palaeolithic in the region, from the Acheulian of the Mindel-Riss interglacial period to the Mousterian at the beginning of the Würm glaciation. Over such a long timespan, the climate, fauna, and flora varied with the climate, which fluctuated from warm periods to cold or extremely cold periods when there was a good supply of reindeer.

Pech II contained hearths dug into the ground, some of them surrounded by fire-reddened stones, proving that Man knew how to make fire during the Acheulian period.

Several scraped chunks of iron oxide and magnesium oxide were recovered from Mousterian strata. Some of them were even cut into a "pencil" shape. In one of the strata, Peyrony and Capitan also discovered a single, crushed skull of a four-year-old child.

❒ The Sarlat-Carsac cycle path 5 kilometres from Sarlat on the Sarlat-Gourdon road passes both entrances to the cave.

**A complex dig**

Just 100 metres from the Pech I and Pech II cave, Pech de l'Aze IV is a major Mousterian site in the form of a bank of earth up against a wall of rock. It was discovered and explored by F. Bordes (centre of the photograph) who uncovered more than twenty archaeological layers, some of them subdivided into several levels. On a site like this one, it is difficult to dig in the same layer over the entire area. Because of this, the dig is conducted one square metre at a time and the data carefully recorded so that they can then be collated on plans and elevations, layer by layer ■

## ☛ LE RÉGOURDOU

The discovery of the site and of the Mousterian grave in Le Régourdou was amusing, to say the least. Some five hundred metres from Lascaux, on the edge of the plateau overlooking the Vézère valley and the town of Montignac, Roger Constant, a resident of the small hamlet of Régourdou, had been assisting Father A. Glory for several years in his studies of Lascaux. He had even provided Father Glory with board and lodging for a while. R. Constant was convinced that there was another entrance to the Lascaux cave, in addition to the one already known about (which was indeed the prehistoric entrance). He began extensive excavations in *(Contd. on p. 20)* front of his small farm. He did not find the entrance to Lascaux but he did find a Mousterian site and a human grave in September 1957.

**A strong jawbone**
Several items were uncovered in the Neanderthal burial site in Le Régourdou, in particular upper limbs, the spine and the sternum, all of them very well preserved. The skull and lower limbs have disappeared. However, the splendid jawbone is impressive for its proportions and the quality of the teeth (Périgueux Museum) ■

The Régourdou site (visible on the spot) is actually a vast rock shelter whose roof collapsed onto the archaeological contents. Following a chance discovery in 1957, the dig was entrusted to two prehistorians, Eugène Bonifay and Bernard Vandermeersch, who worked from 1961 to 1965. Once the rubble from the overhang was cleared, they found several levels of occupation containing Quina-type Mousterian artefacts, mainly scrapers with flaked retouch that dated back to the beginning of the Würm glaciation.
The human burial was in a shallow pit, carefully capped by a flagstone and surrounded by a small wall of rubble. The body lay on its left side, the head facing North, with the knees bent under the chin and the hands raised towards the head. A fairly large limestone flagstone covered the trunk, while stone blocks and sand covered the rest of the burial. All that now remains of the skeleton is a far from negligible number of bones in good condition, including the sternum. Unfortunately the skull has disappeared but the impressively strong jaw has survived, with all its teeth, intact and scarcely worn down (Périgord Museum of Art and Archaeology, Périgueux).
Adjacent to this human burial, there were also dry stone structures containing the skulls and bones of brown bears. A bear cult was suggested at one time, based on earlier discoveries in Swiss and Italian caves, but the idea was sharply criticised by A. Leroi-Gourhan. Carbon dating gave an age of some 45,000 years.

## ☛ LE MOUSTIER

The small village of Le Moustier is flanked by the bayonette-shaped course of the River Vézère as it flows past the superb cliff known as La Roque-Saint-Christophe and through the Vimont Valley that runs down from Plazac further north. There is a limestone promontory here broken up by terraces and shelters set one above the other, and topped by a shallow cave called "Le trou du Bréchou".
The classic rock shelter halfway up the cliff was explored in 1863-1864 by E. Lartet and H. Christy. It was this rock-shelter that later gave its name to the Mousterian period and industry. Ten metres lower, a second rock-shelter was excavated in the early 20th century, first by O. Hauser in 1907 then by D. Peyrony after the French government purchased the site in 1910.
Unfortunately for French archaeology, it was Hauser who, in August 1908, discovered the skeleton of a very young Neanderthal lad which he named *Homo mousteriensis hauseri*. The remains were sold, at a high price, to the Berlin Museum where the skull was put back together at least four times, never with any success. It was believed that the skull had been smashed by bombs during the Second World War but it reappeared a few years later in a laboratory in Iena, in the former East Germany. It might well be studied in greater detail one day, but no reliable information is available on the burial site itself.
However, we do know something about the human occupation of the upper shelter, and even more about the people who lived in the lower shelter, thanks to the digs conducted by

**Le Moustier**
Le Moustier lies at the confluence of the Vimont Valley and the Vézère, on the right bank of the river. The houses in the village are built on rocky terraces in the limestone at the corner of the two valleys. Two superimposed rock shelters have been explored here since 1863 and the industries have been recognised as typical of the Mousterian ■

M. Bourgon and D. Peyrony in 1905 followed by D. Peyrony in 1910. Information was also provided by the study of industries undertaken by F. Bordes and the observations of layers of rock and sediment made by H. Laville and J.-Ph. Rigaud in 1969.

The Mousterian occupation occurred in the first two stages of the Würm glaciation and was followed by brief occupations in the Chatelperronian and Aurignacian at a time when the two rock-shelters were nearly completely filled. At all these times, the accommodation extended well beyond the rocky overhang.

D. Peyrony, and more especially F. Bordes, defined several types of stone tool industries in Le Moustier characterized by tool types and their proportions compared to the tools as a whole. The different shapes do not seem to correspond to different populations but rather to varying activities.

❐ The exterior of the site is open to the public. For a guided tour, book at the visitors centre in Font-de-Gaume: Tel. +33 (0) 553 068 600; email: fontdegaume@monuments-nationaux.fr.

**Stratigraphic sequence in Le Moustier**
Some of the filling from the lower shelter has been preserved and, today, a mould of the layers displayed on the site shows the superposition of several layers from the Mousterian, topped by two layers from the Upper Palaeolithic (Aurignacian then Châtelperronian). The site was occupied between 50,000 and 70,000 and 32,000 years ago approximately ■

plateaux between the valleys. Some, however, lived in rock shelters or shallow caves.

They buried some of their dead in their homes, in organised and sometimes complex graves. They dug out pits, surrounded them with stones or covered them with a stone slab. One of them in La Ferrassie is indented with cupules, bowl-shaped markings. These funereal practices continued and diversified in the Upper Palaeolithic.

About 35,000 B.C., the last Neanderthals were replaced by *Homo sapiens*. For a short period, called the Chatelperronian, the two groups may have co-existed, but they probably did not live in the same groups.

## NEANDERTHAL BURIALS AT LA FERRASSIE

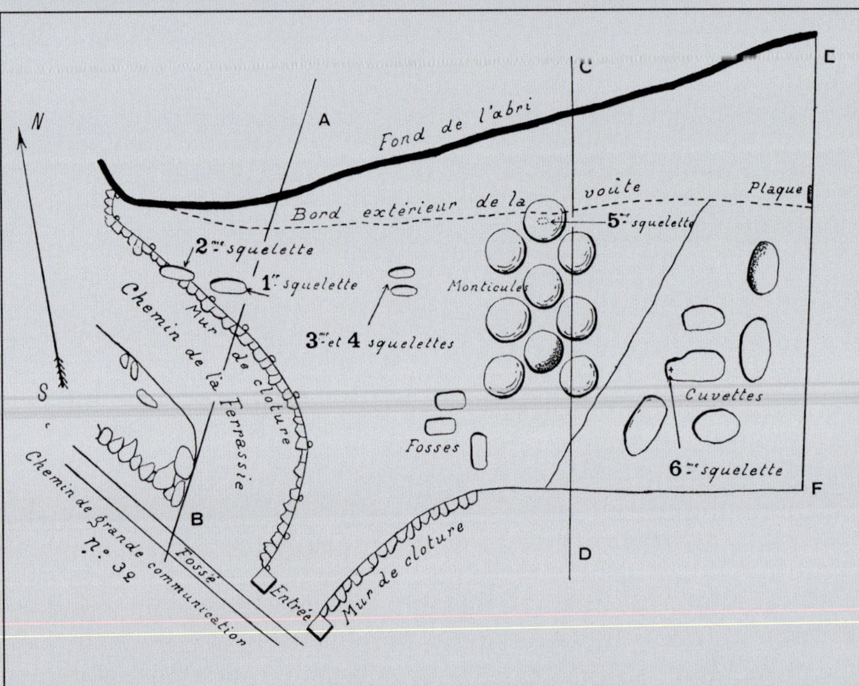


- Beneath the great rock shelter at La Ferrassie between 1909 and 1911, D. Peyrony discovered a number of burial sites, graves and mounds that seemed to form a structured layout.
- On the left were two graves facing in an east-west direction, each containing an adult – a man of between 40 and 45 years of age and a woman aged 25 to 35. In another grave to the right, a 10 to 12-year-old child was buried, and a fourth grave beside it held the remains of a stillborn or newborn fœtus and a 15-day-old baby. In front of the rock shelter were three empty graves and eight mounds. Bones found in one of them, in a depression, belonged to a baby aged approximately 7 months. Finally, one of the six large depressions on the right contained the remains of a child aged approximately 3 years old whose skull lay 1.25 metres away from the body. The head had been severed at the time of burial. Moreover, this grave was covered by a large slab of limestone. Another child, aged approximately 2 years old, was discovered by H. Delporte near the wall of the rock shelter and the mounds.
- This is definite evidence of a funerary rite that was exceptionally complex for its time. It is also unusual for the presence of children ranging in age from newborn up to early adolescence. These Neanderthal remains were studied by Jean-Louis Heim. The adults provided data for a detailed study of Neanderthal characteristics (the male is one of the best examples from this group). The remains of the children have contributed to an understanding of Neanderthal growth and development. For example, it was observed that the skeleton matured much faster than it does today, which accounts for the primitive characteristics.

## ☛ LA FERRASSIE

This site is somewhat off the beaten path, midway between Savignac-de-Miremont and Le Bugue, in a small valley that joins the Vézère at Le Bugue. The large south-facing rock-shelter is at the intersection of the valley and a smaller side valley, just beside the road. In fact, it was the building of the road that led to the site's discovery in the late 19th century. Amateur archaeologists quickly made their way here, including the young schoolmaster from Les Eyzies, D. Peyrony, in August 1896. For thirty-three years, la Ferrassie was his main area of research, conducted by L. Capitan who bought the site in 1923 before bequeathing it to the State.

The roof of the rock-shelter was invisible at the start of the research, because it was masked by a vast bank of earth 40 metres long and 20 metres deep. D. Peyrony's dig gradually reached the rock-shelter's filling i.e. layers from successive occupations and large blocks of stone from a series of roof collapses. By the end of his work, D. Peyrony had succeeded in excavating one hundred square metres of the site and had partially revealed the rear wall of the rock-shelter. He left behind two, six-metre stratigraphic profiles (one longitudinal and the other transversal), clearly showing the accumulation of several archaeological layers.

La Ferrassie is a major site in the region's prehistory. At its base, it revealed well-preserved Neanderthal burial sites and, in its upper section, it illustrated the first stages in the Upper Palaeolithic. It was here, and later in Laugerie-Haute and La Madeleine, that D. Peyrony documented the successive human occupations of Périgord, providing data which was used later by Father H. Breuil to establish, on a much larger scale, his "subdivisions of the Upper Palaeolithic".

**The Great Shelter at La Ferrassie. Stratigraphic sequence**
This large shelter was wide open at the end of the Mousterian and the Neanderthals buried their dead in it. Its canopy then gradually collapsed in the early years of the Upper Palaeolithic. The Mousterian layers are easily distinguishable at the base of the stratigraphic sequence. Above is a succession of Aurignacian and Gravettian occupations, separated by rubble from the collapsed canopy. In the Aurignacian layers were some of the oldest works of art ever discovered ■

Much later again, from 1968 to 1973, H. Delporte again began studying La Ferrassie. Starting from the stratigraphic profiles, to which he gave a more regular form, he dug only a very small portion of the rockfall but he did so very meticulously, providing more detailed knowledge of the site's stratigraphy.

La Ferrassie was the scene of significant discoveries for the Mousterian. From 1909 to 1921, Peyrony uncovered several human burials just above the rocky soil, and a number of corresponding structures.

❒ The exterior of the site is open to the public. For a guided tour, book at the visitors centre in Font-de-Gaume: Tel. +33 (0) 553 068 600; email: fontdegaume@monuments-nationaux.fr.

# The beginning of the Upper Palaeolithic

*In Périgord, modern man appeared some 35,000 years ago and, for 25,000 years until the end of the Würm glaciation, these semi-nomadic hunter-gatherers made perfect use of the resources of the region in which they lived.*

Their period in history, the Upper Palaeolithic, began with Würm III, the coldest phase in the last period of glaciation, and continued until the end of Würm IV. These *homo sapiens* are commonly referred to as Cro-Magnon Man, named after a rock shelter in the village of Les Eyzies where the first fossilised bones of these people were unearthed, in 1868.

**The Cro-Magnon shelter**
This shelter, located between Les Eyzies and Tayac, was discovered in 1868, only five years after the first prehistoric research carried out by Lartet and Christy in Périgord. While building a road, workers uncovered the first known burial site for prehistoric Man classed as "modern man". Dug into the foot of the cliff lining the left bank of the River Vézère, some 250 metres upstream from the Pataud shelter, it is now concealed by the Hôtel Cro-Magnon. This small site, in which the canopy collapsed during the dig, was originally an Aurignacian settlement before becoming a burial site in the Early Gravettian. Human remains (at least three men, one woman and a newborn baby) were found close to the top of the archaeological deposit that almost completely filled the shelter ■

## The Châtelperronians

The transition into the Middle Palaeolithic was embodied in the Chatelperronian civilization (35,000 to 30,000 B.P.), which is known from the Chatelperron cave in Allier. It is clearly defined at La Ferrassie above a series of Mousterian levels and beneath a significant sequence of Aurignacian layers. It can also be seen in the lower rock shelter in Le

**The Vézère Valley in Les Eyzies**
In the Somme Valley, Jacques Boucher de Perthes (1788-1868) realised that prehistoric man had existed and he described "Celtic and antediluvian antiquities". In the Vézère Valley and around Les Eyzies, in 1863, E. Lartet and H. Christy launched the prehistoric research that has turned Les Eyzies into the "Capital of Prehistory" and the Vézère into the "Valley of Mankind" ■

Moustier. During this period, the climate became gradually colder.

This "Mousterian disguised as Upper Palaeolithic", as A. Leroi-Gourhan put it, combined Mousterian type tools, a Mousterian-Levallois knapping technique, and Upper Palaeolithic shapes (chisels and end scrapers). Its best-known tool has a curved back and is called the Chatelperron knife. At this time, the first true bone tools appeared. Most of them were awls but there were also a few sharpened bone and antler fragments. The discovery of the skeleton of a Neanderthal male from the Chatelperronian at Saint-Césaire in Charente-Maritime again gave credence to the notion that this was a transitional civilisation.

The Chatelperronian layers at Arcy-sur-Cure in Yonne are famous for yielding the oldest

**The Cro-Magnon shelter**
This valuable watercolour by M. Féaux shows a cross-section of the Cro-Magnon cliff. It contained two shelters, one above the other. The lower shelter was totally concealed by rock falls caused by the gradual erosion of the limestone rock. Extraction of the stone for the roadway revealed the lower shelter in 1868. It contained skeletons lying in a prehistoric layer at the top of the deposit, accompanied by various artefacts such as flints, shells etc. The upper shelter has now almost completely disappeared (SHAP collection) ■

bone pendants, the oldest bone with paired incisions, as well as Neanderthal teeth. However, more recent studies of the site cast doubt on the appearance of jewellery at that time.

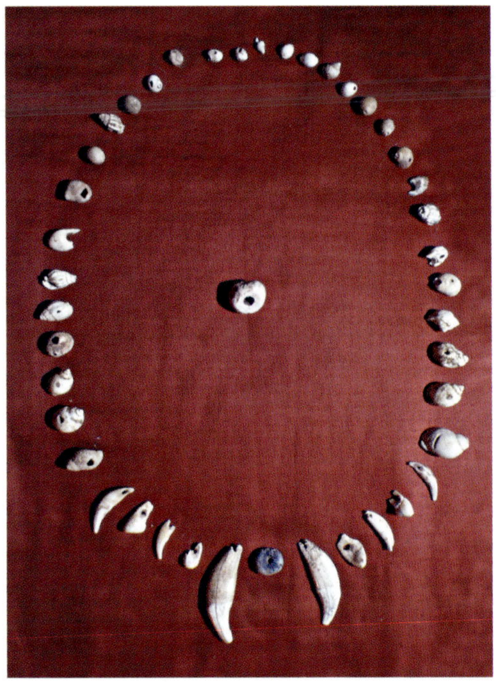

**The Sergeac necklace**
Jewellery developed in the Aurignacian Era. In some of the sites in the Roches de Sergeac Valley (Blanchard and Castanet), there have been numerous wonderful finds, consisting of small items made of bone, ivory and stone, or pierced shells. They were probably sewn onto clothes, stitched to form a sort of net or strung to make a necklace. It is the discovery of such beads by M. Castanet that led to research being conducted in this valley. This necklace is an attempt at reconstituting a piece of jewellery (Sergeac Museum) ■

## The Aurignacians

The Aurignacian Era (35,000 to 25,000 B.P. approximately) brought with it the first significant Cro-Magnon civilisations. It was widespread in Europe (Spain, France, Central Europe, and Italy) and extended as far as the Near East. Digs on several large sites in the Périgord (La Ferrassie, Castanet, and Pataud) are taken as benchmarks by all prehistorians.

The Aurignacians experienced a harsh, dry climate producing steppe-like landscapes alternating with wetter periods during which tree growth increased. Reindeer were the commonest animals with horses and deer when the climate was milder or mammoths and woolly rhinoceros when the temperatures dropped.

The Aurignacians developed implements that lasted throughout the Upper Palaeolithic (end-scrapers, chisels, perforators) but each period had its specialties. In the Aurignacian, end-scrapers accounted for more than 50% of the tools. Blades were thick and sometimes narrow, and were often retouched, resulting in a large number of small flakes. Early Aurignacian (I at La Ferrassie) is associated with split-based bone points, Middle Aurignacian (II at La Ferrassie) with more or less thick lozenge-shaped bone points, and a later Aurignacian (III and IV at La Ferrassie) with thicker bone points.

It was at this time that figurative drawing was born. It was an extraordinary Cro-Magnon invention, which consisted of reproducing in two dimensions what existed in nature in three dimensions. In Southern Germany

**The Aurignacians' toolbox**
In addition to the traditional end-scrapers, chisels and punches used by all groups in the Upper Palaeolithic, the Aurignacians made a whole series of end-scrapers with thick, scaly blades. They also fashioned bone, reindeer antlers and ivory ■

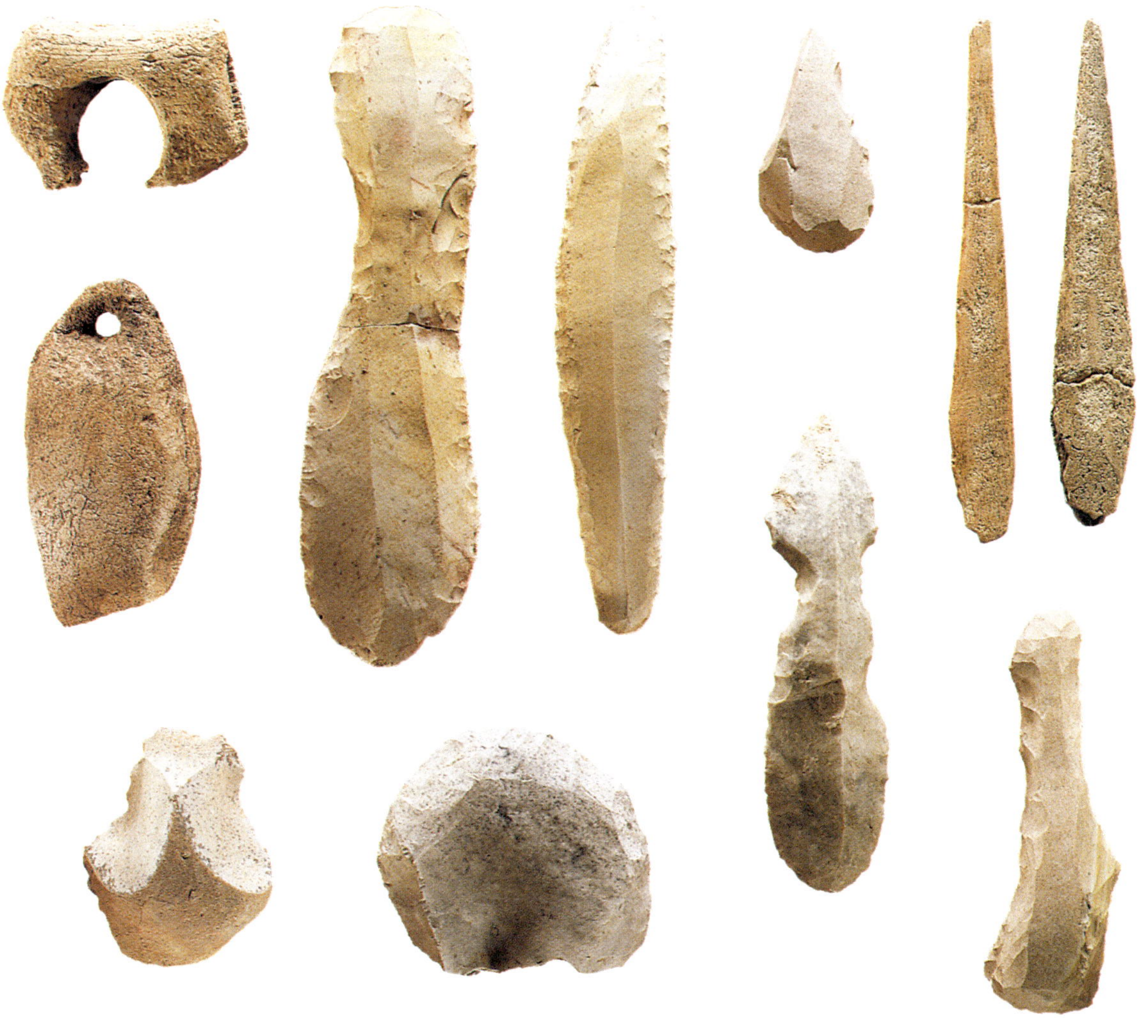

# ART IN ITS INFANCY IN PÉRIGORD

- The Aurignacian shelters around Les Eyzies yielded carved or engraved limestone blocks as well as reminders of everyday life. The drawings usually consisted of female sexual images, rudimentary and often unfinished animals and puzzling geometric signs.

- Moreover, humans decorated the roofs or walls of their rock shelters with designs consisting of painted or engraved lines and applications of colour. However, the extreme cold of the period, led to the deterioration of the walls exposed to the elements and as a result nothing is left of them today. We know that they existed solely because identifiable fragments were recovered from archaeological strata in rock shelters such as Blanchard, Castanet, La Ferrassie and Pataud. In Périgord, very few caves have decorations that date from this period. The ones that do exist are small, with heavily eroded walls upon which an organized system of images can be seen. In Bernous, near Bourdeilles, three rudimentary animals are aligned in a frieze, and in La Croze-à-Gontran at Les Eyzies, panels of animals are separated by geometric symbols. The Cavaille cave in the Couze Valley is decorated with engravings of mammoths, probably dating from the earliest days of the Upper Palaeolithic.

- The decorated blocks of stone from this period can be seen in the National Museum of Prehistory in Les Eyzies, the Museum of Périgord's Art and Archaeology in Périgueux and in the museum in Sergeac.

**A painted rock shelter in pieces**
The Aurignacians from the Blanchard shelter in Sergeac decorated the vaulted roof of their shelter with paintings. However, the roof collapsed as a result of ice (during the coldest period of the Würm glaciation) and the decoration was broken to pieces. On one large fragment of rock, it is still possible to see the very bloated belly and the limbs of an animal, probably a horse, outlined in black on a red background. The remainder of the painting has been lost. The Blanchard rock shelter was studied by L. Didon and his loyal workman M. Castanet, in 1910-1911 (Périgueux Museum)

**An Aurignacian ibex**
The Belcayre shelter is less than a kilometre from the Vallon des Roches, on the opposite bank of the Vézère (right bank), at the foot of a rockfall. During an exploratory dig in 1923 or 1924, F. Delage recognised two Aurignacian levels and M. Castanet discovered a block of stone decorated with a pecked engraving of an ibex. Then the site was completely disrupted. The animal is seen in profile. Its legs are stiff and there is no attempt at perspective. The species is recognisable thanks to a few details i.e. the short tail and small horns engraved on the edge of the stone (Les Eyzies Museum)

**A sculpted phallus**
The Vallon des Roches in Sergeac seems to have been a particularly popular place in the early Upper Palaeolithic. The Blanchard rock shelter on the right bank was occupied by Aurignacians on several occasions (I and II). They have left us some fifteen decorated blocks of stone, a priceless reminder of Man's earliest drawings, depicting female sexual organs (vulvas) and male sexual images (phalluses) as well as animals, all vigorously engraved in limestone. At the base of the site, on the edge of a hearth dating from some 30,000 years ago, the oldest figurative work of art in France was uncovered. It is a phallus fashioned in the bony base of a cowhorn (National Archaeology Museum) ■

(Baden-Wurtemberg), Aurignacians invented sculpture in the round. They sculpted small statues representing animals and human beings. Here, along the course of the River Vézère in Périgord within a 15km radius of Les Eyzies, half a dozen Aurignacian camps beneath rock-shelters yielded the first examples of cave art.

The discovery of the amazing Chauvet Cave in Ardèche, in which the decoration has been so well preserved, showed that, originally, men also decorated large underground sanctuaries with very elaborate designs. However, for the moment at least, they are very rare and nothing like this has yet been discovered in Périgord. The superb engravings in the Pair-non-Pair Cave in Gironde, not far from Le Bec d'Ambès, probably date from these distant days. The animal decoration is very well structured around a light well but is in poor condition because of the type of rock.

**Block engraved with images of vulvas**
Found in an Aurignacian III layer in La Ferrassie, this large block of limestone (56 x 40 cm) has deep incisions representing female vulvas surrounded by several cupules. Other pecked or finely cut lines may be sketches for, or remains of, additional figures (Les Eyzies Museum) ■

**The Pataud rock shelter**
The Pataud rock shelter stretches over one hundred metres or more at the foot of the huge cliff face in Les Eyzies. On the site of the digs undertaken by H. Movius and his American team are two large stratigraphic sequences that clearly show the 14 archaeological layers representing every stage from the Aurignacian and Gravettian to the early Solutrean. The Pataud shelter is a benchmark site for the early Upper Palaeolithic. All the objects have been retained on site and are on display to the public in the museum there. This is the only prehistoric site in Périgord presented in this way ■

## ☛ PATAUD ROCK-SHELTER

The Pataud rock shelter lies 250 metres downstream from the Cro-Magnon shelter in Les Eyzies, on the left bank of the Vézère. It was a farmer, Martial Pataud, who discovered the site at the end of the 19th century, but it was American prehistorian, Hallam L. Movius from Harvard University, who undertook a scientific dig of this exceptional site. Initial soundings were done in 1953 but the main digs were undertaken from 1958 to 1964 and the results published in America over the next 25 years. For the past twenty or more years, the work has been taken over by the Prehistory Department of France's National Museum of Natural History, with new digs during the month of September since 2005.

Two large trenches 9.35 metres deep flank the main dig. They give insight into the passage of time and are as easy to "read" as an open book. This is a former shelter used as a settlement by prehistoric Man for some fifteen thousand years, from 35,000 B.P. Some forty settlements have been found, with remains forming fourteen archaeological levels separated by rockfalls – nine Aurignacian levels, four particularly rich Gravettian levels (early, middle, upper and final), one Early Solutrean and the remains of a Solutrean level with laurel leaves.

An abundance of stone and bone artefacts has been uncovered on this site including jewellery and art objects, traces of cave art, and human burials. In all, almost two million objects have been found. This has become a benchmark for the beginning of the Early Palaeolithic Period.

Behind the old farmhouse, now a research centre, is another very deep shelter, all that remains of the original shelter. On its roof is a superb low-relief carving of a mountain goat. It doubtless dates from the last period of occupation during the Palaeolithic period, i.e. during the Solutrean. The shelter remained in use during the Middle Ages and the front wall bears the date 1734. It now houses the Pataud

Rock-Shelter Museum set up by Henry de Lumley and B. Delluc.
At the base of the cliff, on a level with the main street in Les Eyzies, Mousterians settled on a beach on the banks of the Vézère some 40,000 years ago. The place is called Vignaud.

❐ The Pataud rock-shelter site and museum are open during the summer season: Tel. +33 (0) 553 069 246 and email: pataud@mnhn.fr

**Female form in the Pataud rock shelter**
This is a small block of rock carved with the tiny low-relief outline (58 mm tall) of a young woman. Her arms are not shown and her slightly rounded abdomen indicates the early stages of pregnancy. It comes from Level 3 (Upper Gravettian). At that time, some 21,000 years ago, Man built a real dwelling between the cliff and the fallen rocks. On the ground of this dwelling are hearths, the remains of game, flint tools, jewellery items, numerous objets d'art and even traces of the painted decoration in the shelter (Pataud rock shelter museum) ■

**Statue of Mrs. Pataud**
Some 20,000 years ago, almost the entire roof of the Pataud shelter collapsed, on the site of the digs conducted by H. Movius. The floor of the shelter was then used as a burial ground for 3 adults and 2 children. The skeleton of a young Gravettian girl (aged 16) had been fairly well preserved. She was 1.60 metres tall. A statue of her was made by E. Granqvist, following advice from M-A. de Lumley. She is on display in the museum and is commonly referred to as "Mrs. Pataud" ■

## IMAGINING LIFE IN PATAUD

- The geological and palynological studies indicate a range of climates in which the hunter-gatherers lived, returning over and over again to seek shelter under a rock that has since collapsed. There were periods of intense cold during which vegetation was sparse and periods of more temperate climate. Taking account of these more clement periods, the occupation of the Pataud rock-shelter corresponded to the periods of harshest climates in the Quaternary Era as a whole.
- Developments in the shape of tools over the passage of time reflect cultural changes. A study of even the smallest traces, based on usage, and the spatial distribution of artefacts at a given time provide insight into the life of these men, women and children in their long-term settlements or short-term hunting camps. They reveal how their settlements were structured around their hearths, where they carved a given flint implement, where and how they used it, where they butchered the game that they caught and where they kept their jewellery and art objects etc.

### Ibex in the Pataud rock shelter

This male mountain goat (*Capra ibex*) with its long horns dates from 18,000 or 19,000 years ago. The small head, large abdomen and short, moving limbs are seen on the figures carved in the Solutrean period in the Fourneau du Diable and Roc de Sers (Charente). The front legs are merely juxtaposed, with no attempt at perspective, as are the rear legs. This wonderful low relief was discovered in 1986 on the roof of a surviving section of the Pataud shelter (Pataud-Movius shelter) by B. and G. Delluc with M. Lacoste. The shelter, which was turned into a cellar in the 18th century, is now the Pataud rock shelter museum

**A strange Gravettian Venus**

The Venus from the Facteur rock shelter in Tursac is carved in the round and is 8 cm high. It was made from calcite and was uncovered during stratigraphic work by H. Delporte. The form consists solely of large buttocks and a prominent abdomen suggesting a pregnancy (National Archaeology Museum) ■

**Engraved lines as fine as a human hair**

In the Labattut rock shelter, there was an extraordinary little limestone pebble with very fine grain (10 cm in diameter) decorated with a finely incised and meticulously detailed horse. The style remains archaic (Musée de l'Homme, Paris) ■

## The Gravettians

The Gravettian is the second of the largest civilizations of the Upper Palaeolithic (approximately 28,000 to 20,000 years B.P.). It extended right across Europe from Spain to Russia, but it is in Périgord that the largest number of sites are to be found. D. Peyrony chose the term "Perigordian" to describe this culture and subdivided it into six periods, from I to VI. This terminology has now been abandoned. In digs undertaken up to 1960, the terms Perigordian IV, V and VI continued to be used to describe specific stages in the Gravettian civilisation. An extra, final stage called Perigordian VII or Proto-Magdalenian by D. Peyrony was added, but it was actually the Final Gravettian.

Several famous sites in Périgord were occupied during long periods of the Gravettian, among them the eponymous La Gravette in the Couze valley, and the Pataud rock-shelter in Les Eyzies, in which there was a complete stratigraphic sequence with all the stages of the Gravettian Era (early, middle, late and final).

The climate was very cold at that time, with a few more temperate intervals such as the Tursac interstadial during which trees began to grow again in the best exposed locations.

Flint tools became more diversified and specialized. Chisels dominated (more than 30%), with a large number of truncated chisels and relatively few end-scrapers. La Gravette points are present in every phase in greater or lesser numbers. Small ar-

## GRAVETTIAN ART WORK IN PÉRIGORD

■ In Périgord, cave art was still essentially limited to the walls of rock-shelters and associated with "mobile" art. A remarkable cave in Cussac, discovered in 2000 by Marc Delluc, contains engravings and burials. It dates from the Gravettian, as do the caves in Gargas in the Pyrenees and the Cosquer Cave in Marseille. The traditional techniques of painting (Labuttat shelter in Sergeac) and engraving (Oreille d'Enfer, Pataud and Laugerie-Haute in Les Eyzies) were used but pride of place was given to sculpture (in Laussel and the Abri du Poisson). Animal outlines were usually rudimentary. The beasts were shown in simple profile but the species are clearly identifiable. Sexual acts were depicted, but much less frequently than in the Aurignacian. The female low reliefs in Laussel are particularly spectacular and they correspond perfectly to the form of the many female statuettes called "Venuses" discovered in various Gravettian sites throughout Europe including Sireuil and the Abri du Facteur in Tursac in Dordogne. The Gravettians' mobile art also includes animal figurines, finely engraved pebbles and some decorated tools.

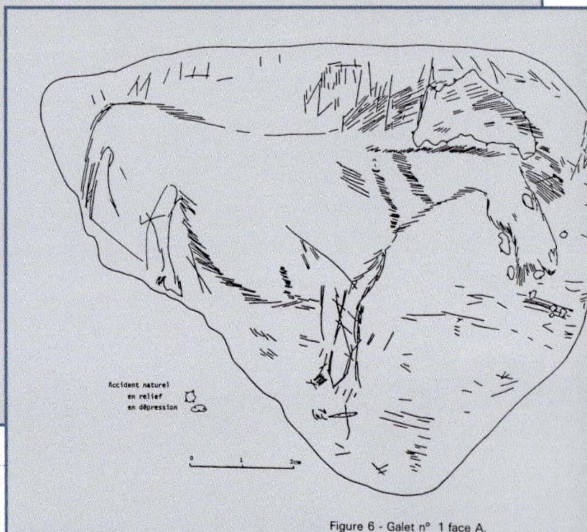


Figure 6 - Galet n° 1 face A.

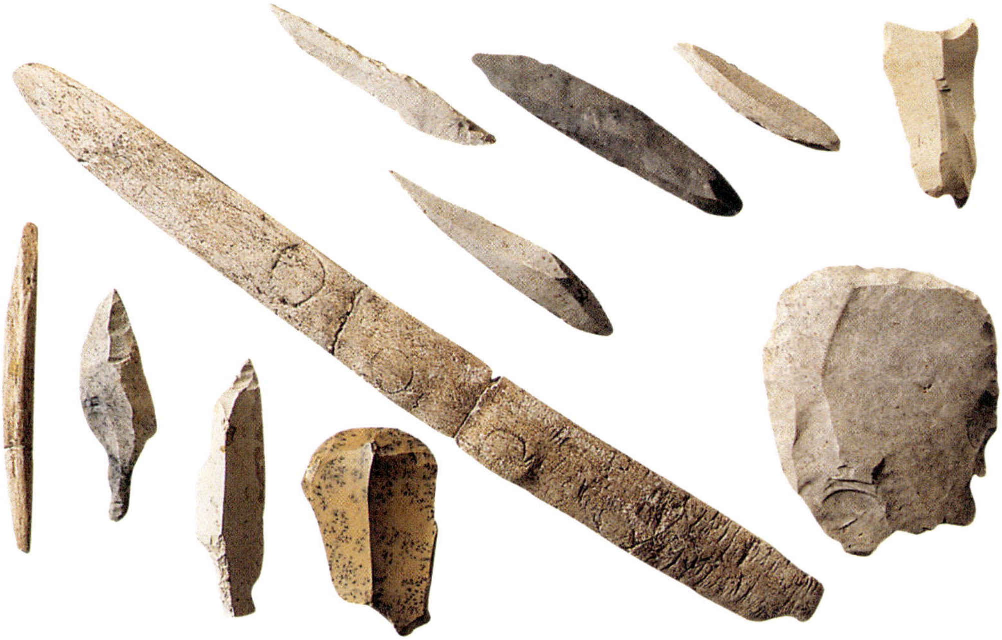

**The Gravettians' toolbox**
In addition to the traditional scrapers and chisels found throughout the Upper Palaeolithic, Gravettian industry is unusual for the La Gravette points, the rectilinear backed bladelets which were designed to be fitted onto handles. Other tools indicate the various subdivisions in this period

rowpoints are found in the Early Gravettian, small Noailles chisels, Font-Robert points and truncated items in the Middle Gravettian and large truncated blades in the Upper Gravettian. In the Final Gravettian, chisels account for 40% of tools and backed bladelets some 30%. Bone tools are always present but are not very characteristic (awls, pierced batons, and bone points) and ornaments are abundant (pierced shell, teeth, bone).

The Gravettians have given us some superb works of art on blocks of stone and some beautiful cave art.

**The couple from Terme-Pialat (Saint-Avit-Sénieur)**
This small low relief has an unusual subject – a couple. The woman (left) is shown in profile. She has large buttocks, an abdomen and drooping breasts. The top of her head is striated. The man (right) is stronger and he appears to have an erect penis (Périgueux Museum)

**Hunter or Amazon?**
Not far from the "Venus with the Horn" in the Laussel rock shelter, a slab of limestone was found, decorated with a carving of a slender figure seen in profile. Is it a hunter or a young woman? (Aquitaine Museum, Bordeaux) ■

## ☛ LAUSSEL

In Grande Beune Valley a few miles upstream from the river's confluence with the Petite Beune stand the Laussel rock shelters, 500 metres upstream from the castle of the same name, on the right bank like the castle, and only a few hundred metres upstream from the Cap Blanc rock shelter opposite Commarque Castle.

The "Great Shelter" (Grand Abri) is over one hundred metres long and lies a dozen metres above the valley floor.

It was explored in the late 19th century and was later intensively and summarily excavated between 1908 and 1914 by an archaeologist from Bordeaux, Dr. Gaston Lalanne. Yet this site was of great scientific value.

The oldest deposits correspond to diverse periods of the Mousterian, followed by the classic succession of Chatelperronian, typical Aurignacian and Gravettian, with La Gravette and Font Robert points. A total of eleven strata five metres deep in all were excavated along an 80-metre trench.

Laussel's fame stems from the discoveries, made in 1911 and 1912, of five sculptures of human figures that seem to be from the Gravettian layer and are therefore more than 20,000 years old.

The most famous, the "Venus with the Horn", was carved on a block of stone several cubic metres in size which had previously fallen to the floor of the shelter. It can therefore be considered as cave art. The other bas-reliefs were carved on limestone slabs 40 to 50 centimetres in length and were found a few metres away. It has been suggested that this site may have been a sanctuary or "*cella*".

The "Venus with the Horn", "Venus with the Gridded Hair" and the "Berlin Venus" are all frontal views of nude women with large breasts, women who have already had several children and are again pregnant. On the other hand, "the Hunter" seen in profile has long been described as a male figure. Yet although the figurine has no breasts, it does not have any male attributes either so it may in fact be a statue of a young woman.

The last block is more puzzling. Two figures, one of them obviously female, are shown lying head to foot. The engraving is pecked, wide and deep. Is it depicting a birth?

Four bas-reliefs are on show in Bordeaux (Aquitaine Museum). The fifth, which was illegally sold to the Berlin Museum by a dishonest field director, was probably destroyed during the Second World War. The only remaining trace of it is a few copies.

**Mysterious Venus of Laussel**

This "Venus with the Horn" is the oldest known low relief representing a woman. She appears young yet she has already given birth and breastfed a child. She is now pregnant again. One hand lies on her swollen belly; the other holds an enigmatic striated cow's horn. Her face is featureless and the hips are rounded. Many other sculptures in the round from the same period also illustrate the notion of motherhood (Aquitaine Museum, Bordeaux) ■

## ☛ GORGE D'ENFER AND ABRI DU POISSON

On the right bank of the Vézère is a small valley known as Gorge d'Enfer. In it, over a distance of less than 300 metres, are seven prehistoric sites dating from the Aurignacian to the Upper Magdalenian.

On the left side of the valley is the Grand Abri ("Great Shelter"), an impressive sight that was once the opening of a cave subsequently reshaped by erosion. Probably occupied during the Magdalenian, it was emptied of its archaeological contents when it was used for saltpeter mining during the French Revolution.

Further down the hill and downstream are two shelters, Lartet and Poisson, carved out of a terrace in the rock. In 1918, D. Peyrony uncovered Early Aurignacian occupation characterized by split-based bone points. It had been preceded by a brief period of occupation in the Chatelperronian.

The adjacent Abri du Poisson was not discovered and explored until 1892 and the sculpture of a salmon on the roof remained hidden until 1912. That year, the Berlin Museum launched a project to purchase the sculpture and the rock surrounding it was cut away. However, Peyrony effectively intervened, the venture was abandoned, and the piece is still in place, albeit damaged by the attempted removal.

The salmon is 1-metre long and piked, i.e. it is male whose lower jaw is curved upward into a hook during the spawning season. The relief is very low and combines raised bas-relief with engraving. The entire object was colored red and some traces of colour are still visible. In front of the fish, still on the vault, a negative of a hand outlined in black paint was discovered just a few years ago.

The dig conducted by D. Peyrony in 1917-1918 brought to light two successive occupations of this shelter – one in the Aurignacian as in Abri Lartet, and the second, in the Gravettian. It is reasonable to assume that the sculpture and the painted hand date from this later period.

Upstream from the Grand Abri is the Oreille d'Enfer, or Chênes Verts, cave. It was subjected to a brief dig in the early 20th century (Gravettien with Noailles chisels and Solutrean).

On a bench in the wall of rock to the right of the cave entrance, several engravings were found beneath the Gravettian layer – two nearly complete does and the head of a third. The engraving was detached from the wall and is displayed in the museum in Les Eyzies.

To the right of the marks left by the removal, six groups of pecked depressions can be seen, combining a large central depression with three to five other, smaller dips. These designs are fairly comparable to those found in the Blanchard, Castanet, Laussel and Poisson shelters (Aurignacian) and are reminiscent of bear paw prints.

❒ The Abri du Poisson is open to visitors with advanced booking at the visitors centre in Font-de-Gaume: Tel. +33 (0) 553 068 600 and email: fontdegaume@monuments-nationaux.fr

**The Gorge d'Enfer in Les Eyzies**
This small valley was inhabited in the Aurignacian and Gravettian periods (Abri du Poisson and Grotte d'Oreille d'Enfer) ■

**A salmon one metre in length**
This Gravettian low relief on the roof of the "Fish" (Poisson) rock shelter is the only known carving of a fish. Just before 1914, the owner tried to sell it to a museum in Berlin and began to cut it away. The subject matter is rare in cave art but more frequent in mobile art forms ■

**The hand of a Gravettian**
On the roof of the Abri du Poisson, this imprint of a hand outlined in pale black is the oldest known "negative" hand in Périgord, with the one found in the Labattut shelter in Sergeac ■

**The deer in Oreille d'Enfer**
This block of stone was removed from the wall of the shelter for debatable conservation purposes. It shows a doe with juxtaposed limbs, without the use of perspective, and the remains of three other deer (Les Eyzies Museum) ■

**The stone decorated with aurochs**
This enormous block of stone measuring half a cubic metre has been carved in low relief. There are two aurochs on the right, another set obliquely in the centre, two horses on the left (they are more difficult to see) and a representation of a vulva in the lower right-hand corner. There are still a few traces of red ochre colouring. The natural perspective is respected. The stone decorated a Solutrean dwelling found in the Fourneau du Diable (Les Eyzies Museum) ■

## The Solutreans

This splendid civilization existed for only a short time and in a limited area (Spain and the southern half of France between the Loire Valley and the Pyrenees) some 18,000 to 21,000 years B.P. It seemed to have appeared suddenly without direct links to the Gravettian civilisation which preceded it in time and it may have originated in the Ardèche region. The Solutreans were talented artists and craftsmen. They produced high-quality flint tools made beautiful by the reworking of all or some of the tools' surfaces. They included unifaced points, laurel leaves, shouldered points, and willow leaf points. They also invented a tool used in everyday life: the eyed bone needle.

The Solutreans were also fine artists. They decorated small caves in the Ardèche Gorge with engravings and drawings (Chabot and Bidon), using red and black pigments. They also made use of graphic artifices that were to become commonplace during the Lascaux period (e.g. cattle horns in twisted perspective).

The Solutrean Period in South-Western France left a particularly large number of rock-

shelters decorated with bas-reliefs, although the art work has unfortunately been badly preserved here. The roof of the intact section of the Pataud Shelter, with its carved mountain goat, is an exception to this. In Le Fourneau-du-Diable near Bourdeilles and Le Roc-de Sers (Charente) between Brantôme and Angoulême, large areas of rock were carved in shelters dating from the Upper Solutrean.

**Bison in La Grèze**
The small La Grèze cave (Marquay), which was once lit by natural light, is decorated with bison, mammoths and megaceros, no doubt from the Solutrean period. The bison is deeply incised and is archaic in appearance, shown in simple profile. The limbs are stiff and have no hooves. There are, however, numerous details in the carving such as a beard, tail, phallus and outline of hooves. Although shown from front view, the horns seem to be incorrectly placed, under the hump on the back of the neck ■

The aurochs in Le Fourneau-du-Diable are highly characteristic of the Solutrean style in this area, with their small heads, prominent stomachs and short legs (and, on one of them, an ear placed in the back of the neck). Natural perspective has been maintained and two aurochs to the right have been superimposed on two levels. From a technical point of view, these carvings resemble a development of the Gravettian sculptures found in the region; stylistically, they are the precursors of the great works of art that were soon to adorn the walls of the cave in Lascaux. This low relief is displayed in the museum in Les Eyzies.

## A LUXURY RESIDENCE

- A remarkable square hut surrounded by rocks and dating from the end of the Solutrean was discovered in the shelter at Le Fourneau-du-Diable. The climate of this period was harsh, cold, and dry, particularly in the Early and Late Solutrean, interspersed with temperate, more humid periods (one of which is best known as the Laugerie interstadial). Reindeer were abundant in the beginning of this period, and were followed later by ibexes and Solutré horses. With the exception of Solutré in Saône-et-Loire, the major sites of this time are located in the Dordogne: Laugerie-Haute, le Fourneau-du-Diable, les Jean-Blancs and Pataud.
- Few objects were decorated during this period, except in Parpallo near Valencia, Spain, which produced engravings on slabs of stone from the Gravettian to the Middle Magdalenian.

**Lignite pendant**
This pendant from Le Fourneau du Diable (Bourdeilles) is one of the few examples of "mobile" art from the Solutrean period. Made from an unusual material (lignite), it bears a fairly rudimentary engraving of a deer. The choice of material shows the Solutreans' interest in uncommon minerals. They are also known to have collected tiny polished pebbles (Les Eyzies Museum) ■

**The skill of flint knapping**
Men in the Solutrean period excelled in the art of knapping, cutting flint to form items in the shape of laurel leaves. The items are thin and sharp and have been retouched on all sides ■

## ☛ LAUGERIE-HAUTE

Laugerie-Haute lies a short distance upstream from Laugerie-Basse. The entire cliff faces South-East and is thus well situated. The shelter, however, is concealed by enormous rockfalls from the cliff during the Magdalenian. Nevertheless there is a vast living space here, 180 metres long and a dozen metres wide, although the area used to extend further towards the valley, under the present road and beyond.

Laugerie-Haute is divided into two sectors (east and west) separated by a bank of earth on which a "castle" was built in the 17th century. The site has belonged to the State since 1921. At its western tip a Neolithic human skeleton was found, buried in the Magdalenian layer (private property).

Explored by E. Lartet and H. Christy in 1863, the site has attracted numerous collectors and profiteers because of its rich archaeological material, particularly the "laurel leaves", spectacular two-sided flint tools. D. Peyrony and his son Élie were able to conduct a scientific dig on the site and publish their results in 1938. Then F. Bordes and Ph. Smith increased our knowledge of the site.

Laugerie-Haute is a very significant site. Its stratigraphy begins where stratigraphies of earlier occupations at La Ferrassie and Abri Pataud end and it would have been rounded off by Laugerie-Basse (middle and upper Magdalenian) if a proper dig had been conducted there. Instead, La Madeleine provides data for the last three phases.

In Laugerie-Haute, forty-two strata and levels were defined including later phases of the Gravettian, the Solutrean, and the first half of the Magdalenian. Magdalenians V and VI were revealed in old collections but nothing remains on site. This vast rock-shelter was intensively occupied for a period of some 10,000 years, corresponding to a succession of climatic phases that were meticulously analysed by Henri Laville.

Laugerie-Haute contains less art than sites like Laugerie-Basse or La Madeleine, but some of the work is of singular interest. The Final Gravettian or Perigordian VII produced a 30 centimetre long gneiss pebble, deeply incised with groups of lines running in several directions, and a pierced stick made from reindeer antlers engraved in light relief with two mammoths fighting. The backdirt from O. Hauser's dig revealed a block of limestone carved with the head of an ovibos, a musk ox with distinctive horns. The musk ox is rarely portrayed in prehistoric art.

❐ The artefacts can be seen in the museum in Les Eyzies. To visit the site, book in advance at the visitors centre in Font-de-Gaume: Tel. +33 (0) 553 068 600 and email: fontdegaume@monuments-nationaux.fr

**The Laugerie-Haute rock shelter in Les Eyzies**
Located on the right bank of the Vézère, it is 180 metres long. It was explored in 1863 by E. Lartet and H. Christy but it was D. Peyrony who conducted the most relevant study of the shelter. At the end of the Middle Magdalenian, the roof suffered a massive collapse, sealing off existing deposits ■

# The days of Lascaux

*This is the start of the great period of the Upper Palaeolithic, significant for the importance of the use of bones, the quality and diversity of the cave art and the variety and quality of mobile art. This is the period of Lascaux.*

## The Early Magdalenian

The Badegoule shelter (Le Lardin-Saint-Lazare) enabled André Cheynier to define the Badegoulian, at the very start of the Magdalenian, 17,000 to 18,000 years ago approximately. Many authors believe that it is a culture in its own right which developed out of the Final Solutrean. It is unusual for the rarity of backed and other blades, for the abundance of flints reworked as scrapers, and for the presence of robust notched chisels and multiple flint punches. The base of spears is chamfered simply, with lancet lines. Bone tools are thick and reindeer antlers have been fashioned by percussion, using an archaic method that was no longer found in the Magdalenian.

This is the start of the great period of the Upper Palaeolithic marked by the importance of the use of bones, the quality and diversity of the cave paintings and the variety and quality of "mobile" objects.

The Magdalenian civilisation stretched right across Europe but, in its infancy, it was limited to the South-West of France and a major site in Spain (Le Parpallo, near Valencia). There are few sites from this period: Laugerie-Haute and Badegoule in Dordogne; le Placard in Charente. The Early Magdalenian is not represented in the site after which it is named, La Madeleine.

The first Magdalenians continued to use the basic tools of Upper Palaeolithic Man – blades, chisels and scrapers. But they also fashioned dihedral chisels, backed blades, small punches, end-scrapers on unretouched blades, and composite tools (end-scraper-chisels, etc.). Bone points had a robust conical base and were decorated with a few engraved

**The blue horse in Villars**
This small horse is now covered with a layer of calcite, giving the black outline a bluish tinge. The horse is shown with its legs extended as if moving, rather like those of the horses engraved in Lascaux, which were worked at almost the same period ■

## ☛ VILLARS

The Villars cave near Brantôme in the north of Périgord is a maze more than 10 kilometres in length, full of magnificent galleries and large numbers of stalactites and stalagmites. The entrance was cleared in 1953 by the Spéléo-Club de Périgueux and it was club members who, in 1958, found the paintings studied by Brigitte and Gilles Delluc. Several chambers were decorated with black line drawings some 18,000 years ago (horses, bison, mountain goats and geometric designs). A transparent veil of calcite gives them a bluish tinge. At the end of the cave is an exceptional piece of art depicting a man fighting a bison, a subject also seen at the bottom of the well in Lascaux. Studies of the calcite and new Carbon 14 dating are currently underway.

The artefacts found in the decorated chambers (flints, bone, reindeer antlers and natural beakers) are on display. A film and a sound and light show within the cave round off the visit.

❐ The cave is open to the public from 1st April to 11th November. Tel. +33 (0) 553 548 236. Email: contact@grotte-villars.com

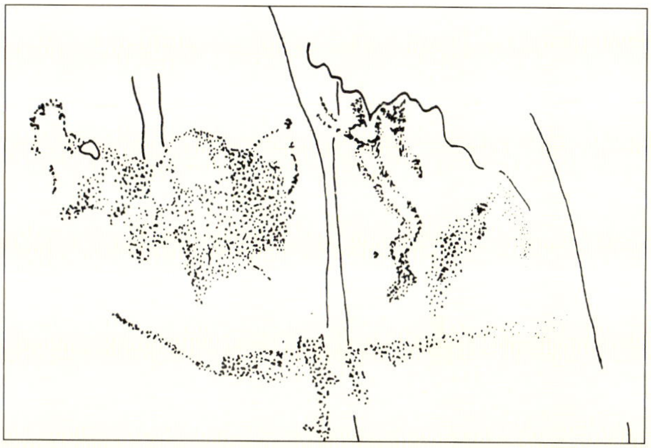

**Villars and Lascaux have their own pictograms**
This is an outstanding piece of artistic narrative – a man with his arms in the air is confronting a bison. A flow of calcite separates the man from the beast and another runs across the bison's back. Only two other fairly similar scenes are known to exist – one in Lascaux and the other in Roc de Sers (Charente). Villars was a sanctuary cave and the scene of the man fighting the bison is the panel the furthest back in the cave, as it is in Lascaux ■

**Jewellery in the ground in Lascaux**
Shells were uncovered in the archaeological layer. Some of them come from the beaches of the Atlantic or Mediterranean; others are fossils from Aquitaine and Touraine. This *Sipho* contains a slit to allow it to be hung. The spirals still contain red ochre. Lascaux even provided archaeologists with a small pebble that had been turned into a shell (Les Eyzies Museum) ■

**A painter's bowl**
The cave in Lascaux contained over one thousand objects. This limestone bowl was used to prepare and hold red ochre. It was found in the narrow Passageway running between the Chamber of the Bulls and the Apse, decorated with engravings and red paintings of horses (Les Eyzies Museum) ■

lines, sometimes set out in a star shape or interlinked chevrons (Lascaux). They had not yet invented the atlatl.

The climate was very mild some 17,000 years ago during the Lascaux interstadial, but it soon became cold and dry.

During the early days of the Magdalenian, the use of tallow lamps (rough stone with a slight depresson or a carefully carved stone lamp fashioned into a container) gave people access further and further underground where they decorated deep-set sanctuaries such as Lascaux, Villars or Gabillou in Sourzac. This marked the beginnings of a Magdalenian artistic explosion, and soon meant an increase in the number of cave sanctuaries and art objects.

## Lascaux

The entrance to Lascaux lies on a hillside overlooking Montignac. It collapsed shortly after the cave was decorated by the first Magdalenians, 17,000 or 18,000 tears ago. The cave mouth, reopened by a falling tree, was discovered on 8th September 1940 by a young boy from Montignac, Marcel Ravidat, when his dog fell into it. Marcel returned four days later with three friends (C. Agniel, S. Coencas, and J. Marsal) to unblock the entrance.

Lascaux cave is only 150 metres long. The Chamber of Bulls and the Lateral Passage were painted on hard, white, calcite walls. The rest of the cave (The Passageway, The Nave, The Apse, The Pit, The Chamber of Felines) was primarily decorated with engravings, and a combination of paintings/engravings and paintings on yellowed limestone and sandstone surfaces.

**The pink sandstone lamp from Lascaux**
This is an outstanding item found at the bottom of the Well. This pink sandstone lamp has been polished. Its handle is engraving with "interwoven" signs that are very particular to Lascaux. The bowl still contained traces of burnt juniper. It was used like our own ancient tallow lamps (Les Eyzies Museum) ■

The floor in Lascaux had only one archaeological layer but its contents, including artists' tools, flint and bone tools, jewellery, lamps, the remains of meals etc. made it possible to recreate a picture of life for those who came to the cave. Pollen was characteristic of the Lascaux interstadial and the carbon 14 dating of charcoal revealed it was 17,000 to 18,000 years old. The flint and antler tools were typical of the Magdalenian II. There were no objects from the Solutrean. Methodical digs would have produced better results, but the floor was excavated to allow for air-conditioning work.

Lascaux cave was a sanctuary. The layout and quality of its images, as well as the objects abandoned by those who frequented the cave, prove that this was not the lair of some magician but rather a kind of cathedral devoted to one of prehistory's religions. Lascaux' artists were professionals who performed a service for the group and for the faith of its members.

## ☛ LASCAUX II AND LE THOT

Since 1983, Lascaux II, a few hundred metres from the original cave, has shown visitors what people used to see in the Chamber of the Bulls and Lateral Passage. The copy of the cave is a ferrous cement shell shaped like, and built to the dimensions of, the galleries in the cave itself. The figures and symbols visible in the original cave have been painted on its walls as accurately as possible. The Centre of Cave Art (*Centre d'art pariétal*) in Le Thot in Thonac also displays the decorated galleries in the Nave and Well and figures of people in movement. It is intended to develop other transportable panels for exhibitions and there is a project to build a new, more comprehensive copy of the cave at the foot of the hill in Lascaux.

❐ For information, contact: Sémitour Périgord, Tel. +33 (0) 553 056 565. During summer, visitors wishing to access Lascaux II must book at the visitors centre in the village of Montignac. Off-season, tickets are available at the site itself. Joint tickets for Lascaux II and Le Thot are also available. Tel. +33 (0) 553 507 044.

**An exact replica – a "Lascaux" horse in the Lateral Passage**
To preserve Lascaux, it had to be closed to the public and a replica was built. It is a true copy of the paintings in the Chamber of the Bulls and Lateral Passage, on reconstituted rock walls close to the cave itself (Lascaux II). Panels from the other galleries in the cave (Nave and Well) are on display not far away in Le Thot. Work is currently underway on other replicas ■

The cave enjoyed enormous success, attracting so many visitors that it was almost lost. Pollution, caused partly by unsuitable air conditioning in 1957-1958, led to the spread of "green algae" on the rock walls. The cave had to be disinfected. The carbon dioxide, heat and water vapor brought in by tens of thousands of visitors each year (120,000 in 1962!) may have caused the proliferation of opaque calcite crystals that eventually concealed the paintings. The dangers of this "white disease" led to the cave being closed to tourists in 1963. A simple process succeeded in recreating the microclimate that had preserved the art for so many years but the installation of another air conditioning system in 2000 led to further infestation and treatment is posing serious problems.

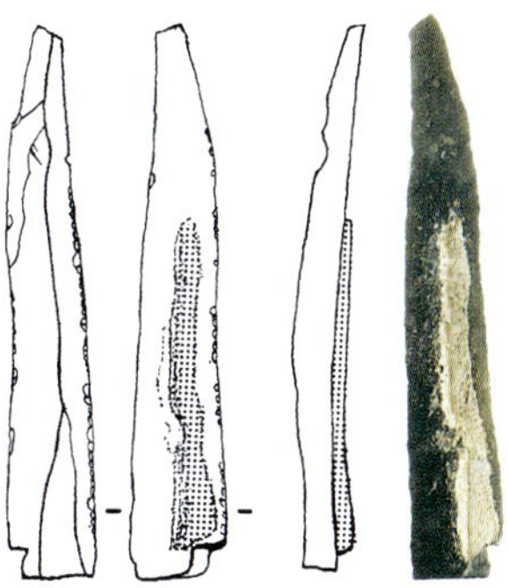

**The mastic used for flints in Lascaux**
Some of the tools from Lascaux bear traces of a mastic used to fix them to handles. The mastic is thought to have been made of resin and powdered ochre. The small flint blades were set into handles to create, for example, spear tips (Institut de Paléontologie humaine) ■

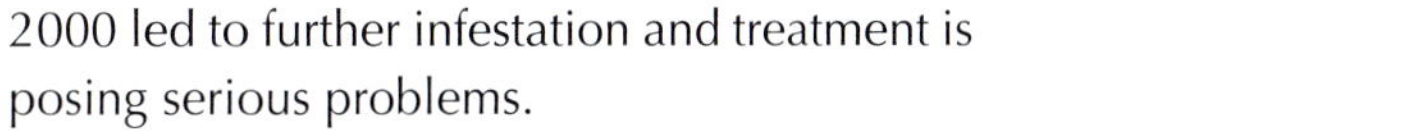

**An engraved spear from Lascaux**
The spear tip bears the image of a 6-branched star similar to signs found on certain walls of rock. The items found in the only archaeological layer in the cave, which dated from the early Magdalenian, therefore belonged to the artists (Les Eyzies Museum) ■

**Lascaux: horses, aurochs and stags**
The combination of a large bovine and several smaller horses is a sort of leitmotiv in the art in Lascaux and is no doubt full of symbolic meaning. However, the significance of this particular painting has been lost. Signs and stags complete this work in the Chamber of the Bulls ■

**Lascaux: bison in single file**
These two male bison in the Nave comply with the stylistic conventions of Lascaux.
Perspective is suggested – the bison on the right is behind the bison on the left.
The front bison has lot some of its coat due to the summer moult.
The attitude of the two animals can be seen in the natural environment during the mating season ■

**Lascaux: Bull no. 2 in the Chamber of the Bulls**

This 3.5 metre long auroch is characteristic of the style used in painting cattle in Lascaux. The head is seen in profile and the horns from a three-quarter view, with an ear in the back of the neck. The enormous body is seen in profile and the chest from a three-quarter view. The legs are short and moving. The hooves are seen from front view

### Lascaux: a strange story

Unlike the others, this scene in the Well seems to be telling a story. A bison has been eviscerated and is losing its entrails yet it is charging a rudimentary human (bird's head, hand with four fingers, erect penis). The animal is stiff. Its head is set at an unnatural angle and it is beating the air with its tail, giving a slight sense of movement. In the lower section of the work, there is a bird (possibly at the top of an atlatl), a sign like barbed wire and a long line that may be a spear. Further left is a woolly rhinoceros and, on the opposite wall, is a horse ■

## THE MESSAGE FROM THE CAVES: AN ONGOING RIDDLE

■ Palaeolithic Art is not anecdotal. The animals, human figures (these are rarer) and signs that form the art works in these cave sanctuaries, do not tell a story. They are mythograms whose meaning has been lost because no information was handed down by the person who originally created them. A few pictograms are still comprehensible today e.g. the scenes showing a man and an ox (Lascaux, Villars, Le Roc de Sers), mountain goats locked in combat (Lascaux), mammoths (Rouffignac), the two bison placed rump to rump in Lascaux, or a few other ethological scenes which show that the cave artists were also hunters, with excellent knowledge of the anatomy and behaviour of animals.

## Lascaux: the Jumping Cow

In the Lateral Passage, this female auroch 1.27 metres long is shown in movement. Her rear legs are bent at a forced angle while her front legs are extended. Her tail is spiralling to form a whip. In front of her is a quadrangular sign with numerous tiny horses underneath. They have small heads, bloated abdomens, short moving legs and rounded hooves. In fact, they resemble the Prjewalski horses we know today, which originated in Asia ■

**Lascaux: in single file**
These five paintings of stags' heads in the Nave in Lascaux, each approximately 1 metre in height, form a frieze. The artist must have climbed up a bank to reach this panel. The animals are already old and they form a group of stags like the ones seen in the natural environment. The antlers are set out in a traditional manner, one in front of the other. The ears are also painted in a fashion typical of Lascaux – one of them is on the back of the neck and the other is set against the side of the neck. The first four stags are drawn in black (manganese dioxide); the last one in brown (clay from the cave) ■

## Art in Lascaux

The decoration in Lascaux is particularly structured. It is like a cathedral, with themes carefully distributed across the available space and completed by a language based on geometric symbols whose meaning is still not understood. The art in Lascaux is very unusual. Animal anatomy and behaviour have been carefully observed but the hand of the artist has transformed what the eye of the hunter has seen. The outlines have been systematically distorted, with small heads, large bodies, short moving limbs, horns seen from a three-quarters view and hooves seen from above.

There are three types of symbol in Lascaux – large rectangles, most of them divided into sections, like the famous "coats-of-arms"; lines with side branches (a star with six branches, a St. Andrew's Cross, lines with one or more barbs or interlinked chevrons); and one or two rows of punctuation marks.

In the Middle and Upper Magdalenian, a few thousand years after Lascaux, art became much more realistic and less unusual than the

## THE WORK OF THE ARTISTS

- The Lascaux cave was studied by Father André Glory from 1952 to 1963. He traced the 1,500 engravings decorating the galleries. He conducted a dig on the floor of Well, collecting and describing the numerous artefacts left here by the Magdalenians. He died accidentally in 1966 and the results of his research were published for the first time in 1979 (*Lascaux inconnu*, edited by Arlette Leroi-Gourhan). His manuscripts and the many artefacts he owned, which disappeared after his death, were found thirty years later and published in 2008 by Brigitte and Gilles Delluc.
- Observation of the cave walls and the building of Lascaux II revealed the techniques used by artists in Lascaux. The paintings were done with manganese dioxide (black) and natural ochres (yellow, brown and red). The pigments were applied using the fingers, brushes made of animal or plant fibres, or wads of fur or fibres. Sometimes liquid pigments were blown onto the surface from the mouth. The outlines, some of which are very sharp, were obtained using skin stencils. Pigments came from "pencils" of ochre or manganese, which were either used directly on the rock or scraped to produce a coloured powder set onto the wall of rock thanks to the lime-bearing water.
- The engravers used flint tools with strong points or shards of bone to cut into the rock. The points of these artefacts are worn. Numerous figures in the Nave are a combination of engraving and painting. Paintings of Lascaux have been published in countless well-illustrated books.

work seen in Lascaux, but the symbols nevertheless remained frequent and enigmatic. The artistry of the great hunters of France and Spain, the art work visible in rock-shelters and caves, died out some 10,000 years ago. The art came to light again elsewhere in Europe, on rocks in the open air (Arctic, Alps, Spanish Levant, Sahara, etc.) where it was often more diagrammatic than the work dating from our Palaeolithic age and full of representations of human figures.

**Lascaux: a "coat-of-arms"**
In the Nave, three large rectangular signs divided into sections appear close to a large black cow and horses. Other similar signs can be seen here and there on the panels in the cave but the ones in the Nave are both engraved and painted in patchwork fashion. Their meaning remains a mystery ■

# The Upper and Middle Magdalenian

*The Magdalenian, at the end of the Upper Palaeolithic some 16,000 to 13,000 years ago, was the greatest civilisation of the prehistoric era. It was the Age of the Reindeer.*

## The Middle Magdalenian

Father H. Breuil defined six subdivisions based on the shape of the flint and, more particularly, the bone tools. The Middle Magdalenian corresponds to stages III and IV; the Upper Magdalenian to stages V and VI. Some authors prefer to link stage III to the Lower Magdalenian and stage IV to the Upper Magdalenian.

The Middle Magdalenian was marked by a cold phase which lasted for two thousand years, followed by a relatively milder climate. In the first phase, large numbers of reindeer, horses and saïga antelopes lived in the steppe-like grassy landscape. In the second phase, horses increased in number, while the antelope population decreased radically or disappeared altogether. The climate became milder and more humid. Tree cover increased and even included deciduous trees.

Magdalenian stone tools were fairly unremarkable with the usual procession of end-scrapers and chisels, often combined on the same blade or associated with other tools. Tiny retouched bladelets were quite numerous and were sometimes either denticulated or triangular.

Stage III is characterised by bone points which are often short and thick, with a single bevel, and generally with a longitudinal groove in the back. Semi-cylindrical antler segments also emerged at this time, often with either no decoration, or decorated with incised geometric signs. Pierced batons, smoothing tools, notched bone, needles etc. have also been found.

In stage IV, bone points have single or double bevels, are sometimes striated but no longer have dorsal grooves. Antler segments are engraved or decorated with motifs in relief. Reindeer antler points also appear with lateral notches. These are often described as harpoon prototypes. There are also small, thin, perforated bone disks bearing geometric decorations or animal representations. Hooked atlatls were made from reindeer antler or ivory, and were occasionally decorated with impressive animal carvings. The number of engravings on bone, ivory, reindeer antler, stones, pebbles, or slabs increased significantly in this period.

Well-defined at Laugerie-Haute, the Magdalenian III is also present at Cap Blanc, Rever-

**The headless women**
The last Magdalenians drew very realistic animals and, sometimes, very simplified outlines of women consisting of no more than the torso and buttocks. This woman is engraved on a block of stone found by F. Bordes in La Gare de Couze, in a layer dating from the Magdalenian VI (Les Eyzies Museum). There are known to be several such engravings in a number of sites and caves in Périgord (Lalinde, Fronsac and Font-Bargeix) and elsewhere ■

dit, Raymonden, Gabillou and in some open-air sites in the Isle Valley. The Magdalenian IV was present in the lower stratum of the site of the same name, and at Laugerie-Basse and Raymonden.

## Upper Magdalenian

With the end of glaciation fast approaching, large Quaternary animals such as the woolly mammoth and rhinoceros, as well as the migrating reindeer, began to disappear. This period, between 13,000 and 11,500 years ago, was marked by a last bitter resurgence of cold temperatures in the Magdalenian V, followed by another cold but more humid period which gave rise to denser forests in the Magdalenian VI. Reindeer were still present, but deer, roebucks, wild boars, and aurochs appeared or increased in number and constituted the new fauna for the temperate periods to follow.

These last two stages of the Magdalenian are usually defined by the shape of harpoons made from reindeer antlers, whereby the Magdalenian V has unilaterally barbed harpoons and the Magdalenian VI harpoons are bilaterally barbed. These objects served as the heads of harpoons. In other words, they were detachable weapons that were fitted onto a wooden haft. An unravelable cord probably enabled the user to recuperate the spearhead and the harpooned prey. These objects often have widened bases which may have facilitated the tying of a rope and prevented it from slipping. Some more recent harpoons were even perforated for this very purpose.

The last stage of the Magdalenian also saw the emergence of new flint tools, notably parrot-beak chisels, points with semi-abrupt lateral retouching (Laugerie-Basse points) and some with peduncle (Teyjat points). An increasing number of other forms was also developed, later serving as the basis of the Azilian industry. Such implements included Azilian points with curved backs and abrupt retouches, small and short end-scrapers, finely retouched geometrically-shaped microliths, and a few flat harpoons from the extreme end of the Magdalenian. The latter were still made from reindeer antler and preceded the Azilian harpoons made from red deer antlers.

This powerful culture was well represented in the Périgord and left behind works of art, mostly engravings, on cave walls (Teyjat), blocks of stone (Limeuil) and a number of other small objects such as bone, reindeer antler and stone. The artwork shows rare artistic quality. Some of them are real miniatures; others are strangely deformed drawings of horses or reindeer with disproportionate heads. There are also other, very schematic or stylized pieces, notably the profiles of female figures.

## Magdalenian sites

Périgord boasts countless rock shelters that were occupied in the Magdalenian era and they have often been used to define the chronology of the period. Some of the outstanding artefacts found in them are now on display in the largest national and international museums.

**Fishing or hunting?**
Magdalenian harpoons are usually made of reindeer antler and have rows of barbs on one or two sides. They probably fitted into wooden hafts that could be thrown using atlatls. Nobody knows whether these weapons were actually used for fishing or hunting (Périgueux Museum) ■

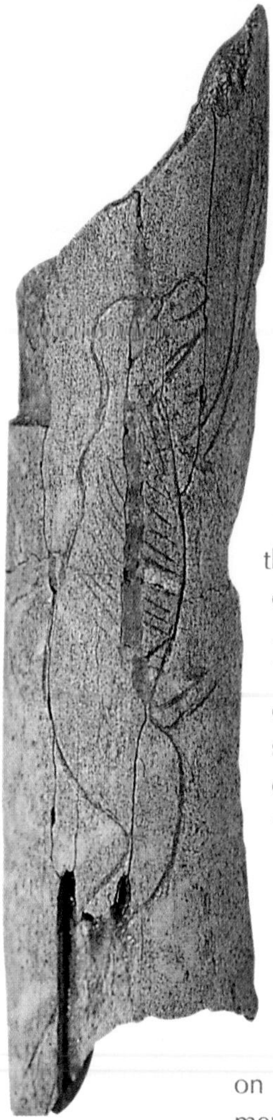

**A man with a beast's head**
Discovered at the bottom of the site in La Madeleine (Magdalenian IV), this fragment of bone is decorated with an engraving of a human figure that is obviously a man. The head is like a caricature – it resembles a beast or perhaps a mask. There are other similar engravings, notably on a pebble found in the same archaeological layer (Les Eyzies Museum) ■

## ☛ LA MADELEINE

Explored in 1863-1864 by E. Lartet and H. Christy, La Madeleine is a vast rock-shelter at the base of a cliff on the right bank of the Vézère in Tursac, just downstream from a side meander.

The excavated area of the site is 50 metres long and 10 to 15 metres wide. Lartet and Christy conducted a dig in the central section. In May 1864, they uncovered a portion of mammoth tusk decorated with the engraving of a mammoth. The accuracy of the drawing shows that it was created by a person living at same time as the animal. The lithic and bone industries from La Madeleine led G. Mortillet to designate this site as the reference site for the last period of the Palaeolithic. In 1872, he coined the term "Magdalenian".

The site is difficult to reach and was relatively undisturbed until 1910, when D. Peyrony conducted a number of methodical digs. They ceased at the outbreak of the First World War. He was able to distinguish three superimposed layers, based on variations in the stone and bone implements discovered there.

Father H. Breuil used this information to define the last three stages of the Magdalenian (IV, V and VI). The first three had been defined in Le Placard (Charente).

In 1926, D. Peyrony discovered a child's grave and he published information on the site in 1928.

Abandoned for several decades, research began again in 1968 under the direction of Jean-Marc Bouvier. It defined the stratigraphy and included a number of analyses and carbon 14 dating.

The animal species found at La Madeleine give some indication of the food preferences

**An outstanding site.** In its lower reaches, the River Vézère forms numerous meanders. Slightly downstream from Tursac, it forms an almost closed loop before flowing past the cliff at La Madeleine. At the foot of the rock, on the left, is the shelter that gave its name to the Magdalenian period ■

**Villepin, another Magdalenian site**
This rock shelter near La Madeleine was occupied during the Magdalenian VI and the Azilian. This small piece of schist is decorated with a fairly realistic horse's head. It was used as a compressor or retouching tool for flint implements (Les Eyzies Museum) ■

of prehistoric populations. In almost every layer, reindeer account for 87 to 100% of the remains; only one layer from the end of the Magdalenian IV contains a mere 63% reindeer, while horse make up 36% of the remainder. It appears that other species including ibexes, bison, oxen, chamois, and roebucks made up a very small percentage of the Magdalenians' diet. Note that reindeer were not only a source of food, but also provided skins to make tents, bedding, and clothing, as well as bones and antlers to make needles, awls, bone points or harpoons. Their gut and tendons were used as ligatures. La Madeleine was also an important site for prehistoric art. Hundreds of engraved or sculpted objects originated here. They ranged from the modest to the most spectacular. Many of them are on show in the museum in Les Eyzies and in the National Archaeology Museum in Saint-Germain-en-Laye.

❐ The actual site is not open to the public but there is an interesting exhibition at the visitors centre in the mediaeval troglodyte village. Tel. +33 (0) 553 463 688.

**Ancient digs in rubble**
The digs conducted in La Madeleine since the one undertaken by E. Lartet and H. Christy in 1863 seriously disrupted the site. In 1910, D. Peyrony discovered a large slab of limestone engraved with a splendid reindeer with a very expressive head (National Archaeology Museum) ■

**La Madeleine: a pierced stick**
Since the Aurignacian, pierced sticks had probably been used to straighten the naturally curved spear tips made from reindeer antlers. The beam and the base of the tine on a reindeer antler have been pierced to make a hole that is the active section of the tool. Here the handle is decorated with large-headed horses (Les Eyzies Museum)

**La Madeleine: a bison licking itself**
This small engraving in the round was probably the carved section of an atlatl. The Magdalenian artist has skilfully represented the eye, nostril, ear and horn, as well as the bristle on the mane and dewlap. The attitude of the animal is also well executed. It is shown turning its head and poking out its tongue (Les Eyzies Museum)

**A very dangerous dwelling: the Marseilles rock shelter**
The bottom of this elevation dates from the Middle and Upper Magdalenian. In the Magdalenian VI, the roof consisting of large slabs of rocks one metre thick, collapsed. Then other Magdalenians created a dwelling here on top of the rocks and, much later in 2,700 B.C., they were followed by Neolithic Man. Other rock falls occurred, forming an impressive pile of boulders ■

## ☛ LAUGERIE-BASSE

A tall cliff more than 500 metres in length overlooks the River Vézère flowing some 60 metres below. Fifteen metres above the valley floor, erosion carved out rock-shelters that were inhabited in various prehistoric periods. Later, the houses of the hamlet of Laugerie-Basse were built into one of these shelters.

Digs were conducted from 1863 in the main rock-shelter, which was then a farm. Labourers dug trenches, or even tunnels under the buildings. With Lartet and Christy, other people came to the site for half-a-century, attracted by its immense richness, especially its many works of art. The onslaught of visitors seriously destroyed the integrity of the site and the precise origin of many of the artefacts is unknown.

In 1912-1913, D. Peyrony and Jean Maury explored a small area of the rock-shelter.

Thanks to patronage of the famous chemist, Joseph-Achille Le Bel, J. Maury was able to dedicate several years to digs in a shelter located some fifty metres upstream, the Marseilles shelter. He left a significant site intact.

The original shelter was occupied from the Magdalenian III to the Magdalenian VI and possibly, briefly, in the Azilian. Remains from

**The woman with the reindeer in Laugerie-Basse**
Discovered by Father Landesque in 1867 or 1868, this fragment of bone is engraved with a woman and a reindeer. The size of the belly shows that the woman was in the last stages of pregnancy (National Archaeology Museum) ■

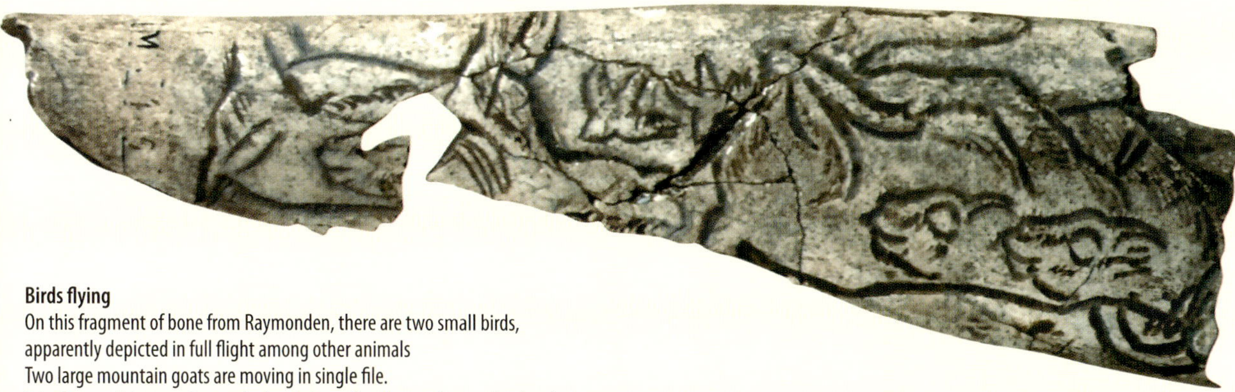

**Birds flying**
On this fragment of bone from Raymonden, there are two small birds, apparently depicted in full flight among other animals
Two large mountain goats are moving in single file.
It is also possible to make out the head of another ibex and two other heads of young mountain goats or cattle (Périgueux Museum) ■

**The ibex disc**
Perforated discs of bone, usually taken from the shoulder blades of herbivores, have been found in several sites, most of them dating from the Magdalenian IV. This one comes from Laugerie-Basse.
It is intact and shows a grazing animal on each side, standing on one and lying down on the other.
A number of authors believed they were mountain goats, or one goat and one doe (Périgueux Museum) ■

the Neolithic and the later Bronze Age were also found in the bank outside the shelter's overhang.

More is known about the occupation of the Marseilles shelter due to the control section, which is still visible. The Magdalenians settled on the shelter's natural floor 14,000 years ago and remained there until the Magdalenian VI, when a large section of the overhang suddenly collapsed, strewing rocks over part of the settlement. Yet the Magdaleians returned, leaving a few traces of their occupation on top of the rockfalls. The shelter was then abandoned until the arrival of Neolithic people from the Artenac culture *circa* 2,700 B.C. A layer of ash and charcoal was dated to this period, covering the entire excavated surface of the rock-shelter. The cliff then collapsed further, leaving behind an impressive rockfall some 8 to 10 metres high.

Laugerie-Basse is famous mainly for its wealth of Magdalenian art. The "immodest Venus", "the Woman and the Reindeer", and many others are especially well-known. All of these pieces are now dispersed across the globe, many of them at the museum in Les Eyzies, the National Archaeology Museum and the British Museum.

❒ The site is open to the public. Tel. +33 (0) 553 069 270. Sémitour Périgord, Tel. +33 (0) 553 056 565.

## ☛ RAYMONDEN

Just upstream from Chancelade to the north of Périgueux is an 800-metre stretch of cliffs that were intensively quarried for stone. The prehistoric site was discovered in March 1876 by M. Hardy, future archivist and curator of the Musée du Périgord. The site was then left untouched until 1887 and the building of the small railway line from Périgueux to Brantôme. The bank in Raymonden provided ballast and cut flints and bones appeared all along the track. M. Hardy and Maurice Féaux conducted a methodical dig there from October 1887 to October 1888.

In his monograph published in 1891, Hardy divided the 1.35 metre-thick "archaeological layer" into four "living floors", each separated by thin layers of sand or clay. Unfortunately, the objects in the Périgord Museum bear no indication of the subdivisions. Overall, they correspond to the Magdalenian IV, V and VI. Among the works of art discovered in Raymonden, one of the most famous is the "Bison Plate".

At the base of the site was the grave of a young man, lying on his left side in a tightly flexed position, with the left hand under the head and the right hand under the chin. As was often the case in the Upper Palaeolithic, the body had been sprinkled with iron oxide, which gave the bones a reddish tint.

Anatomist Léo Testut studied the remains and determined that they constituted a particular fossil type or Homo sapiens race that differed from Cro-Magnon and Grimaldi. These men were fairly small, approximately 1.60 metres in height, and similar to the Inuit with elongated skulls, high straight foreheads and long wide faces. However, these comparisons were later abandoned and the notion of "race" has itself been dropped. The different characteristics of one fossil compared to another are now based on individual variations.

**The bison plate from Raymonden**
This is a fragment of rib from a large herbivore, split to make it thinner. It is 87 mm in length. The plate was perforated at the left end and was probably worn as a pendant, i.e. vertically. A bison's head, two separate legs and seven small human figures create a strange scene. One of the people seems to be carrying a forked stick. The barbed line behind the head of the bison is a mystery. The combination of bison and stylised humans can be seen on another engraved bone from the castle in Les Eyzies, again dating from the Upper Magdalenian (Périgueux Museum) ■

A further dig was started in 1927 by Louis Didon then, in 1928-1929, by Jean Bouyssonie. Four new layers corresponding to Magdalenian I, II and III were then identified. This meant that Raymonden would have been the only site in which it would have been possible to study the six successive subdivisions of the Magdalenian Period if the series of earlier digs had been preserved one layer at a time.

❐ Between two small quarries on the roadside is the small Raymonden cave and its prehistoric site. Collections of artefacts from the site are on display at the Périgord Museum in Périgueux. Tel. +33 (0) 553 064 070.

## ☛ ROCHEREIL

**A perforated, engraved baton**
The site at La Peyzie near Rochereil revealed a few decorated objects from the Upper Magdalenian. This perforated baton, made from a reindeer antler, shows a triangular vulva and, on the handle, a strange drawing, possibly of a plant (mould, on display in Brantôme Museum) ■

This cave is small, only 10 sq. metres in size, on a terrace that widens out to the front, on the right side of the Dronne Valley. M. Féaux and the Marquis de Fayolle conducted an initial dig here in the early 20th century and it almost cost one of them their lives in a rockfall. The most extensive research, however, was carried out by Dr P.-E. Jude between 1935 and 1939. He went on to publish his results in 1960.
Two cultures were identified in the stratigraphy and each was subdivided into several levels. One belongs to the Magdalenian VI, well defined by its stone and bone tools including numerous parrot-beak chisels, Laugerie-Basse points, Teyjat points, bilaterally barbed harpoons, and numerous works of art in a style typical of this phase in the Magdalenian.
The second culture was Azilian and contained a rich collection of points typical of this period along with flat harpoons made from deer antlers. A human grave and charred remains of two adolescents from this period were also found.

The site is adjacent to Rochereil mill, near the small town of Lisle. The artefacts are preserved in the museum in Brantôme.

**A strange animal in the Magdalenian layer in Rochereil**
What species does this strange head on a long neck belong to? What is the meaning of the small decoration engraved lower down? Is this a crested bird, drawn rather crudely, or an imaginary animal? (Brantôme Museum) ■

## ☛ LIMEUIL

The site explored in the early 20th century extended under the houses, gardens and narrow streets of the small town, on limestone slopes overlooking the confluence of the Vézère and Dordogne rivers. It was discovered during earthworks. The dig was conducted by a prehistorian from Brive named Jean Bouyssonie between 1909 and 1913, and covered a distance of thirty metres along a slope below two outcrops of limestone. It is, therefore, an open-air site for the most part.
The culture belongs to the Magdalenian VI, characterised by an overabundance of chisels, including several parrot-beak chisels and bilaterally barbed harpoons. Carbon 14 dating of a reindeer antler suggests a date of 11,720 ± 120 B.P. The engravings on bone and reindeer antler are characteristic of this period. They include beautiful perforated batons decorated with reindeer with disproportionately large heads compared to the bodies, fish and, on other pieces, bison, horses and even a fox, a species rarely depicted in prehistoric art.
The unusual feature of the Limeuil site is the abundance of engraved limestone slabs, plaques and blocks – amost 300 of them have recently been published by Gilles Tosello. Li-

**The last hunters in the Vézère Valley**
Limeuil was home to the last great hunters from the Age of the Reindeer and to the last artists of this era. Numerous small and larger slabs of rock have been discovered under the buildings of the town, engraved with reindeer and other animals

**The last reindeer**
In Limeuil, reindeer are the most frequently depicted animals. On cave walls, however, there are few, if any, such engravings. The animals shown there are not the ones included in the Magdalenians' diet (Périgueux Museum)

meuil was seen by some as a "prehistoric art studio" rather than a centre for portable art. Some of the works are of unusually high quality and stylistic uniformity, with drawings of almost photographic realism in the anatomical details, the proportions of the animals and their movement. They include a reindeer grazing with its head bowed, reindeer rutting, a herd of deer, one of them with its head raised and on the alert, galloping horses etc. On several occasions, a line drawn at the animals' feet seems to indicate the ground, a feature that is rarely depicted in Palaeolithic art. Here, as in Teyjat, red deer and reindeer are the most common animals (60), followed by horses (40). There are also three aurochs, two mountain goats, two bears and one bird.

**A horse in Limeuil**
This is typical of the style of engraving in Limeuil (Magdalenian VI): an almost academic realism that is very different to the style in Lascaux five thousand years earlier (National Archaeology Museum) ■

Limeuil, at the point where the River Vézère flows into the Dordogne, marks the end of the "royal progress" through Prehistory that has taken us from Lascaux to Limeuil, and in a distance of thirty kilometres, covered more than five thousand years in time. The decorated blocks of stone are now in several museums in France and the USA. Some of them are on display in the museum in Périgueux.

**Art on a block of stone**
In Cap Blanc, a bison facing to the right was carved onto a large piece of limestone. It lay at the foot of the wall of rock, in the archaeological layer (Aquitaine Museum, Bordeaux) ■

## The decorated caves and shelters of the Magdalenian

Around Les Eyzies, there are many decorated rock shelters and caves dating from the Magdalenian and eight superb sites are open to the public. The Villars Cave is an exception. Located in the north of Périgord, it is slightly older, dating from more or less the same period as Lascaux. The Mairie Cave in Teyjat in the north of Périgord is only open from time to time.

## ☛ CAP BLANC

The Cap Blanc rock shelter in Marquay is located halfway up the sloping right bank of the Grande Beune Valley, almost opposite Commarque Castle. In the early 20th century, it was just a small cliff at whose base one of those working on the Laussel dig noticed a small crevice, a sign of a probable rock shelter. He began to dig on behalf of Dr. Georges Lalanne. The site was almost fully dug in just four months, from September to December 1909, over a length of fifteen metres and a width of three or four. On the wall at the rear of the shelter, the labourer noticed an animal frieze carved in high and low relief.

The monumental work was studied by Alain Roussot. The only thing similar to it is the carved rock shelter in Le Roc-aux-Sorciers in Angles-sur-l'Anglin (Vienne).

Of the fourteen animals depicted here, six are horses, all except one facing to the right. The one exception, and it is the most spectacular of the carvings, is in the centre of the shelter. It is two metres long. In two cases, the animals are superimposed, with the head of one animal on the rump of the next. There are also three bison, one with its head carved where a horse's head should be. A fourth bison was carved on a huge fallen rock in the shelter (it is now in the Aquitaine Museum in Bordeaux). A bear's head and two reindeer can also be seen here. Traces of red ochre suggest that the frieze was originally in colour.

A study of the stone and bone tools from Cap Blanc, preserved at the Musée de l'Homme and at the Musée d'Aquitaine, attributes the two main layers of the site and the animal frieze to the Middle Magdalenian (Breuil's Magdalenian III). Digs by D. Peyrony and, later, A. Roussot show that the site was also occupied briefly during the Upper Magdalenian.

**Horses stand out from the rock**
In Cap Blanc, the Magdalenians carved an extraordinary frieze on the wall of their dwelling, visible to all. Palaeolithic art is often concealed in caves

A human grave was discovered at the very base of the archaeological layers. It contained the skeleton of a young woman, about twenty years of age, who was laid on the left side in a flexed position. The heels almost touch the pelvis, and the right hand covers the face. Three stone slabs were placed over the body. The skeleton currently on show in the rock-shelter is in a different place from where it was discovered and the skeleton itself is a modern copy, since the original was sold by the owner of the site to the Field Museum in Chicago.

Thus, a single rock-shelter, Cap Blanc shows a direct link between daily routine, funerary ritual, and splendid works of art which were possibly linked to the religion and rituals of the Magdalenian people.

❒ The site is open to the public with advanced booking at the visitors centre in Font-de-Gaume : Tel. +33 (0) 553 068 600 and Email: fontdegaume@monuments-nationaux.fr

**The great horse in Cap Blanc**
The horse is shown life-sized and in strong low relief. It has been carefully finished and was once painted with red ochre. It has lost its limbs as a result of erosion

**The cliff at Saint-Cirq**
These rocks on the right bank of the Vézère have been used as dwellings from the Magdalenian up to the present day. The Magdalenian cave is tucked into the cliff ■

OPPOSITE
**Portrait of a Magdalenian in Saint-Cirq**
Engraved at the back of the cave is the figure of a man with an erect penis. His face is fairly realistic, unlike the few examples of humans engraved in the Palaeolithic era. He is often called "The Wizard" but there is no solid basis for this nickname ■

**The dappled horse in Saint-Cirq**
In the entrance gallery to the cave, there is a group frieze showing a carved bison and four engraved horses. On this one, the coat appears to be dappled. The style is similar to the one seen in Lascaux, dating from the very early Magdalenian ■

## ☛ SAINT-CIRQ CAVE

Located on the right bank of the River Vézère, between Les Eyzies and Le Bugue, the little cave in Saint-Cirq known as the "Sorcerer's Cave" opens midway up the rocks.

The engravings were discovered in 1952-1953 by A. Glory, R. Constant, E. Jardel and B. Pierret, acting on information from B. Mortureux. The cave, which was studied by B. and G. Delluc, is divided into two sectors. On the walls in the entrance gallery are a bison and four horses; on the domed roof at the back of the cave, a man with genitalia surrounded by a triangle resembling a vulva, a bison's head and the head of a mountain goat. On the adjacent wall is a profile engraving or a man fighting a horse and a diagrammatic female figure.
Since the visit by A. Leroi-Gourhan in 1958, and given their styles, the engravings in the entrance gallery have been attributed to the Early Magdalenian and those in the back of the cave to the Middle Magdalenian. This is compatible with a dig conducted nearby that uncovered a remarkable carving in the round of a tortoise.
❐ The site is open to the public from Easter to 1st November (Tel. +33 (0) 553 071 437).

**The Vallon des Roches**
Beneath the Castelmerle promontory in Sergeac, a small stream flows between the rocks down towards the Vézère. Man lived here from the Aurignacian (Blanchard and Castanet rock shelters) to the Gravettian (Labattut shelter) and the Magdalenian (Reverdit shelter) ■

## ☛ REVERDIT SHELTER IN THE ROCHES VALLEY

In the Vallon des Roches in Sergeac, below Castelmerle, two rock-shelters were occupied during the Magdalenian. The first, La Souquette, is located on the left slope of the small valley, facing the River Vézère. The second, the Reverdit shelter, is on the same side of the valley, only 300 metres upstream.

The second of the shelters gets its name from Alain Reverdit, an employee of the Tobacco Department, who discovered it in 1875. Beneath the rock-shelter, which at the time was being used as a byre or sheep pen, he dug into what was left of the archeological layers. Later from 1911 to 1914, Franck Delage reopened the dig in front of the rock-shelter, realising that the prehistoric occupation had also extended towards the valley floor. The two recognised layers of archeological deposits were defined as Magdalenian III, just as at Cap Blanc. There were also engraved blocks of stone and fragments of the decorated cave wall.

It was in 1923 that the site's owner, Marcel Castanet, noticed the remains of carvings on the roof of the shelter. Unlike Cap Blanc, the carvings are in a fairly poor state of repair and they occupy only part of the roof, on the right-hand side. They include a horse, two bison and the outline of the back of a third animal.

In the left (or upriver) section of the site, a sloping bank abuts the cliff face outside the rock-shelter and covers the remains of archaeological layers recently explored by A. Roussot. Several hearths appear in the control section and another one was uncovered at its foot. It is oval in shape and surrounded by large river pebbles placed on their sides.

Some of the artefacts are in the local museum in Sergeac; the others are in the museum in Les Eyzies.

❒ The decorated shelter is open to the public from Easter to the end of September (Tel. +33 (0) 553 507 970).

❒ Starting from the reception area at Castelmerle, visitors can tour the Aurignacian and Gravettian sites in the Roches Valley (Blanchard, Castanet, Labattut, la Souquette), as well as visiting the museum in Sergeac.

**A carved shelter in the Vallon des Roches**
In the Reverdit shelter there are three carvings of bison and only one of a horse whereas in Cap Blanc there are six horses and two or three bison. Yet all the work was done by Magdalenians in the same period ■

## ☛ BARA-BAHAU

At the back of this large cave overlooking Le Bugue, Maud Casteret and her father Norbert discovered a remarkable set of engravings in the soft, flint-rich rock in 1951.

The engravings, which have been studied by B. and G. Delluc, form three rows on the back wall. On the lowest row are two or three quadrangular symbols, three horses, a bear, a reindeer and a bison. Above them are two horses and an auroch while, on the top row, are a horse, a bison and a phallus.

The engravings overlay ancient scratches left by bears and integrate some of these marks, especially on a hand and the coat of a horse. Standing on their own at the end of this long, wide gallery, the engravings suggest a culture similar in style to the Early Magdalenian. The quadrangular symbols are reminiscent of the ones in Lascaux and the tectiforms those of the great caves of Les Eyzies.

❐ The site is open to the public from February to the end of the year (Tel. +33 (0) 553 074 458).

**A horse in Bara-Bahau**
In the Mousterian, bears scratched the very soft rock dotted with pieces of flint. This Magdalenian horse was engraved with a flint; his head was marked out with a finger. Breath seems to be steaming from his nostrils. The mane is erect. He is being followed by another horse. Is this a stallion and his mare? ■

**The bear in Bara-Bahau**
The bear is left-facing and is in a central position, which is unusual in decorated caves. It is a brown bear. A piece of flint is used as the eye and breath seems to be coming from its mouth. The body is represented by the roundness of the rock. On its side is a large pentagonal sign ■

**The auroch in Bara-Bahau**
The auroch is facing to the right. The horns, coat and beard have been depicted using finely engraved lines. The animals in Bara-Bahau are similar to the ones in Lascaux, a combination of horses or bison with aurochs indicating a warmer climate or with reindeer indicating the intermittent persistence of lower temperatures ■

## ☛ FONT-DE-GAUME

In H. Breuil's words, Font-de-Gaume deserves to be ranked among the "giants" in cave art. The cave had been common knowledge among local people for years. The schoolteacher in Les Eyzies, D. Peyrony, knew about it and, three days after his trip to Les Combarelles, on 11th September 1901, he came back for another look at the rock walls and discovered "exquisitely beautiful paintings". H. Breuil and L. Capitan arrived on 15th September. Over several years, Breuil would return to Les Eyzies for months at a time where, sometimes assisted by Peyrony, he set about recording the paintings and engravings at Font-de-Gaume and Les Combarelles. The monograph on the former was richly illustrated in colour and published in 1910. The latter was published in 1924.

The cave was dug into a limestone hill overlooking the right side of the valley, on the left bank of the River Beune. The main gallery is 120 metres long and more or less straight. Three side passages branch off it.

The main paintings and engravings, some of them damaged by graffiti or layers of calcite, are located in the second half of the main gallery, just before the tapering passage named "the Rubicon", and continue to the end of the tall but narrow passageway.

The cave in Les Combarelles is filled with engravings of horses; Font-de-Gaume contains depictions of bison. There are some 85 of them, along with 50 horses, 35 mammoths, 18 reindeer and other deer, 8 aurochs, 6 goats, 2 rhinoceros, 2 felines, 1 wolf, 1 bear, 1 human and 2 vulvas. In addition to this, there are 22 tectiforms and 4 negative hands i.e. only the outlines of the hands are coloured.

Many of the paintings are two-tone or polychrome and many of them overlay an engraved outline. In several places, especially for bison, the natural relief of the cave wall was used to suggest certain parts of the animals such as the head, hump or legs.

The animals are not randomly distributed. Some are paired, such as two reindeer facing off against each other. Others are portrayed in single file or organized in several rows. Some species occupy special positions. High on the cave wall, a wolf faces the intersection of the main gallery and third side passage. There is a painting of a rhinoceros in the last side pas-

**The entrance to the sanctuary in Font-de-Gaume**
The right-hand passage leads to the Magdalenian sanctuary. The left-hand gallery runs for only a few metres ■

**OPPOSITE, TOP**

**Font-de-Gaume, the Bison Cave**

Horses predominate in Les Combarelles; mammoths are the most frequently illustrated animals in Rouffignac. Here, in Font-de-Guame, bison account for almost one-half of the animals depicted. This large male is represented by a combination of fine engraving and polychrome painting, emphasising details and certain features of the animals. The Palaeolithic bison with large horns (*Bison priscus*) has now disappeared ■

**OPPOSITE, BOTTOM**

**In the Bison Chamber**

This area at the end of the cave in Font-de-Gaume contains an amazing concentration of animals, including this bison. It contrasts with the other parts of the cave where the animals are shown in a line. However, many of the figures here are covered with a veil of calcite ■

**ABOVE**

**A strange sign in Font-de-Gaume**

The pentagonal outline of this "tectiform" is reminiscent of a house. Some people have described it as a trap. In fact, it is a sign whose meaning is unknown to us. Other painted or engraved tectiforms can be seen in Bernifal, Les Combarelles and Rouffignac. They are ethnic markers from the Middle Magdalenian found in the area around Les Eyzies ■

sageway, and an engraving of a feline at its very narrow end.

A study of the styles and overlays shows that the work was completed in several stages; one, more or less contemporaneous with Lascaux in the Early Magdalenian, and the other, in the later Magdalenian as found at Les Combarelles, Bernifal, and Rouffignac.

❒ The site is open to the public with advanced booking at the visitors centre in Font-de-Gaume: Tel. +33 (0) 553 068 600 and Email: fontdegaume@monuments-nationaux.fr

The Combarelles cat
This feline (a lion with no mane or a lioness) is drawn with a rhinoceros. The head of a deer can be seen looking up, at the bottom left ■

## ☛ LES COMBARELLES

The cave at Les Combarelles was discovered on 8th September 1901 by the young Father H. Breuil, schoolteacher D. Peyrony and Dr L. Capitan.
Only five decorated caves were known about at that time, including La Mouthe, discovered in 1895, and Pair-non-Pair (Gironde), in 1896, but a number of archaeologists still remained sceptical.

**Deep in a valley**
In the depths of Les Combarelles valley behind a modest farmhouse is a long, narrow, winding passageway decorated with Magdalenian engravings ■

The discovery of Les Combarelles and Font-de-Gaume a few days later was significant. In May 1902, É. Cartailhac made amends by publishing his "mea culpa of a sceptic". In August that year, a committee of experts visited the three decorated caves in Les Eyzies and acknowledged that the paintings dated from prehistoric times. Numerous other explorations revealed several new caves in Périgord, the Pyrenees and Spain.
From 1891 to 1894, prehistorian E. Rivière conducted an extensive, and successful, dig at the cave mouth and in the gallery on the right, the so-called "Combarelles II" where several engravings were found in 1934.
The main gallery, Combarelles I, is 240 metres long. It is a narrow passageway with eleven bends and averages a metre in width but widens periodically at elbow level. After its discovery, the floor level was lowered to improve access; before that visitors had to crawl through the passage.
Various animals are depicted here e.g. reindeer, mountain goats, mammoths, rhinoceros, bears, felines and wolves. The commonest animal is the horse. There are over one hundred of them, one-third of the total according to H. Breuil and C. Barrière. They are followed by bison, aurochs, bears, reindeer, mammoths and, last but not least, deer.
There are many human or anthropomorphic drawings among the paintings of animals, and the vulvas and stylised female figures are very reminiscent of the engravings in Lalinde or Couze (Upper Magdalenian). To all this must be added the symbols, in particular the tectiforms like the ones in Bernifal, Font-de-Gaume and Rouffignac.

In very recent times, speleologist Marc Delluc accessed the end portion of the gallery and found further engravings.

The style of the work suggests that it dates from the Middle Magdalenian according to A. Leroi-Gourhan but some of it may be more recent. A section of a layer from an archaeologial dig conducted in 1973 at the entrance to the gallery provided two carbon 14 dates. The oldest date was 11,730 B.C., while the youngest was 9,430 B.C.

❒ The site is open to the public, with booking at the visitors centre in Font-de-Gaume : Tel. +33 (0) 553 068 600 and Email: fontdegaume@monuments-nationaux.fr

**A beautiful reindeer in Les Combarelles**
This is a reindeer, its head lowered. It has a large muzzle, a projecting shoulder and huge curved antlers. There are some fifteen reindeer here, unlike other decorated caves. Yet reindeer provided Magdalenians with so much food. Like the mammoths (approximately fifteen), though, reindeer give way to horses (more than one hundred), bison (forty or more) and even bears (twenty) ■

**Schematic female figures in Les Combarelles**
The cave contains fifty or more illustrations of complete or partial human bodies (heads, vulvas, negative hands).
The most spectacular are the schematic female figures like these, without heads or feet.
Their massive projecting buttocks (cleft here by a vertical line) contrast with their small chests and slender legs ■

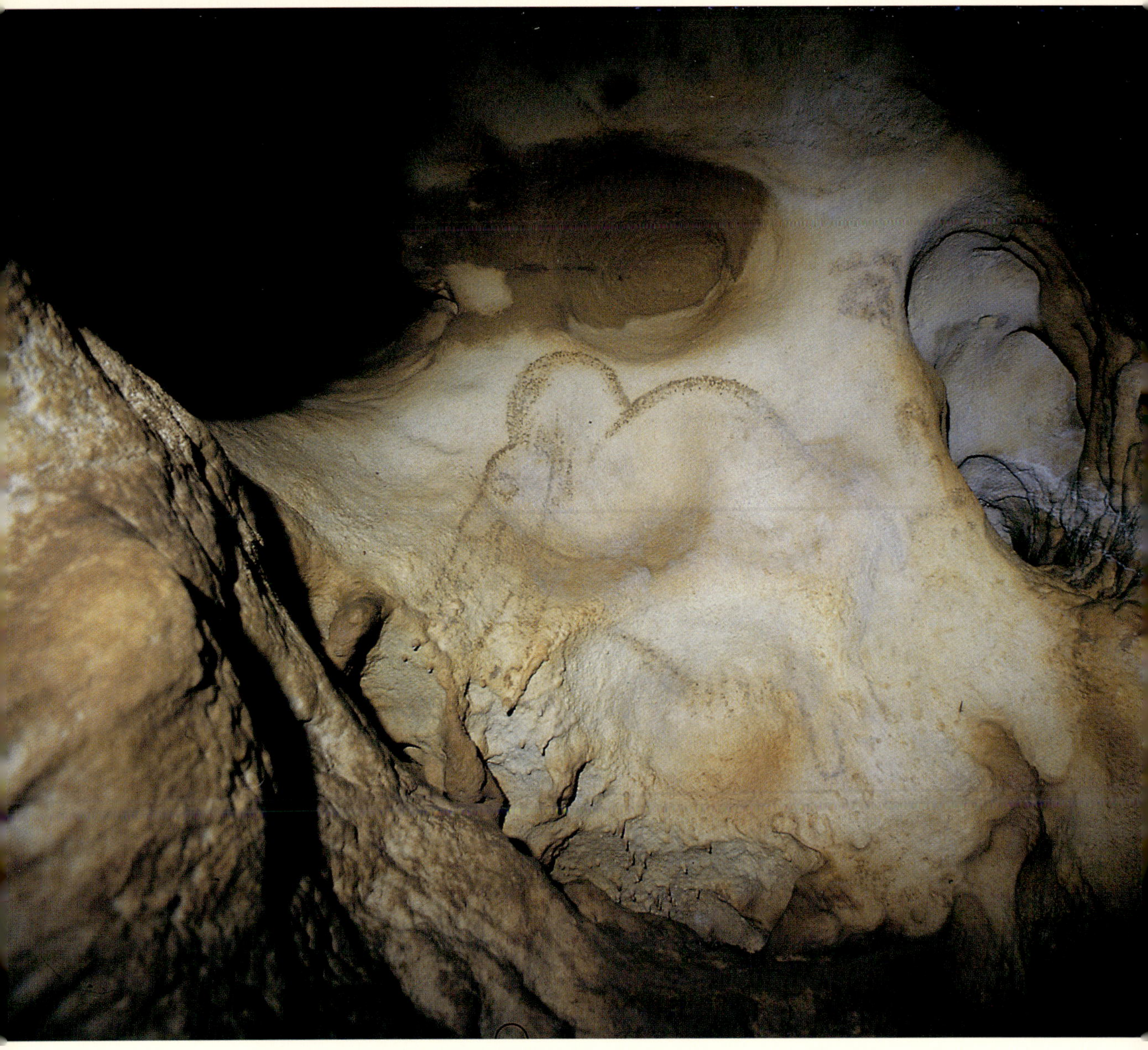

**The hidden mammoth and mask in Bernifal**
These figures were not recognised until one hundred years after their discovery, at the top of an almost inaccessible chimney. The style is amazingly similar to the one seen in Rouffignac. A human face with eyebrows, eyes, nostrils and mouth can be seen on the right, straddling a rocky ridge

## ☛ BERNIFAL

The Bernifal cave lies on a hillside on the left bank of the Petite Beune, just downstream from the Vieil Mouly manor on the road from Les Eyzies to Sarlat.

In 1902, D. Peyrony entered the cave through a small opening in the roof.

The cave comprised two main halls, separated by a very low, narrow passageway. Several small side passages, some of them very narrow and difficult to access, lead off the sides of the second chamber. They, too, contain engravings and paintings.

Like Rouffignac, but to a lesser extent, Bernifal is a cave of mammoths – they account for more than one-half of the fifty depictions of animals found thus far. Most of them are engraved but some are painted, including one that rivals the very best mammoths in Rouffignac. The sense of style is obvious, if lacking in skill. Eight horses, including one ass, seven bovines (bison and aurochs), and two deer complete the list of animals featured in the cave. Three human faces and engraved or "negative" hands are quite remarkable.

Bernifal is also a cave of tectiforms. Although the symbols are shaped like a roof, they are probably not depictions of housing. There are thirteen of them here, twelve engraved and one painted using a series of small, juxtaposed dots. Some of the engraved tectiforms stand alone; others are in pairs, and still others accompany mammoths. One animal that is absent here is the rhinoceros, usually found with mammoths in other decorated caves in the region.

❒ The site is open to the public (Tel. +33 (0) 674 963 043).

**Tectiform signs in the Bernifal Cave**

In normal light (left), one can discern the general shape of the painting, but when photographed on infra-red film (right), it is clear that the painting was made using a very organized series of small, juxtaposed, and evenly distributed dots ■

**The panel at the entrance to Bernifal**

The first figurative drawings in the Bernifal cave are grouped together on a piece of rock projecting from the wall. The relief is immediately reminiscent of a bison's head and is completed by details outlined in red. They include a large round eye, a muzzle and, possibly, a horn. Above the bison, drawn in red, is the outline of a mammoth and to the right, drawn in black, is a human face seen from the front ■

## The Great Ceiling in Rouffignac

Near a well leading to the lower level in the cave is the Great Ceiling decorated with 63 drawings of animals. With the exception of the bear, all the species known in Rouffignac are depicted here e.g. mammoths, bison, horses, mountain goats and rhinoceros. The horses and goats are set out in a circle while the mammoths appear to be more scattered. This group is all the more surprising given that the ground was originally only 60 cm from the roof, preventing any overall view of the work

**The Mammoth Cave**
Rouffignac is often described in books as the "cave of one hundred mammoths". Actually, it contains more than 150 of them. Drawn with black outlines or incised into the rock, some of them stand alone, others are in pairs (often locked in combat) while still others are in groups of ten (two opposing herds). This is a particularly detailed mammoth called "The Patriarch" ■

**A dangerous herbivore**
The woolly rhinoceros, a contemporary of the mammoth, is depicted eleven times in Rouffignac. This one is part of the outstanding frieze showing three of them in a line, each of them very realistic. There are very few pictures of these animals but in Périgord they feature in Lascaux (the scene in the Well), Villars, Les Combarelles and Font-de-Gaume ■

## ☛ ROUFFIGNAC

The vast cave in Rouffignac lies within a limestone hill containing large quantities of flint in the Binche Valley 5 kilometres to the south of the town of Rouffignac and 7 kilometres from the Vézère as the crow flies.

Rouffignac was the subject of what is probably the oldest known description of a decorated cave. In his "Cosmographie Universelle de tout le monde" (1575), F. Belleforest mentioned "paintings and drawings of animals". Over the last century, it was described in tourist guides as a place of interest. The Spéléo-Club de Périgueux reported and photographed the Rhinoceros Frieze in 1948 yet the prehistoric drawings were not discovered until 1956 when, at the request of Ch. Plassard, two prehistorians from the Pyrenees, Louis-René Nougier and Romain Robert, visited the cave and located them.

To the present time, 254 engravings or drawings with black lines have been recorded, including four human figures. This "cave of one hundred mammoths", as it is called in the tourist guides, in fact contains 158 mammoths, which constitute 70% of the animals depicted in the cave. These are followed, in order of frequency, by 28 bison, 16 horses, 12 mountain goats, 11 rhinoceros, and a single bear. Thus, only six animal species are represented, but one of them in unusually large numbers. In the other caves (except Chauvet in Ardèche and Margot in Mayenne), there are no more than one or two drawings of rhinoceros.

There are few symbols here. Fourteen tectiforms and six serpentiforms, finger-painted wavy lines that resemble serpents, have been recorded. Other signs include meandering finger-painted "macaroni" shapes that cover the equivalent of five hundred square metres of wall and, more especially, roof.

The Magdalenians undoubtedly made great use of the cave but they have not left any material traces of their presence here, with the exception of a single piece of worked flint.

As in Lascaux and a number of other decorated caves, Rouffignac suggests its use as a sanctuary and art as a means to express spiritual or possibly religious concepts.

With no archaeological material and no direct dating of pigments, all of them mineral-based here, the style of the art has been used to date the work, which is reminiscent of the Middle Magdalenian tectiform caves in Les Eyzies. The great uniformity of style and technique suggests a fairly small group of artists from the same culture working within a well-defined time span.

❐ The cave is open from March to October and visitors tour it on a small electric-powered train. (Tel. +33 (0) 553 054 171).

**The last bison**
The engravings in Teyjat are cut into flows of amber-coloured calcite which allowed for very finely-executed drawings. This very realistic bison has one anomaly. The artist made a mistake and his "correction" can be seen in the lines of the head. It has created a "shadow" like the ones seen in photographs containing movement

## ☛ LA MAIRIE CAVE IN TEYJAT

La Mairie cave lies on the outskirts of the village. Only the first fifteen metres were occupied during the Magdalenian.

It was in 1903 that D. Peyrony discovered the slender engravings on a film of amber-coloured calcite covering stalagmite formations. Some were on the walls themselves; others on fragments of rock. A dig conducted in 1904 by Pierre Bourrinet, a primary teachr in Teyjat, led to new discoveries and a detailed study of the area at the cave mouth in which people had lived. There were two distinct archaeological layers separated by a sterile layer of rubble. The older layer dates to the Magdalenian V, characterised by unilaterally barbed harpoons. The upper layer is from the Magdalenian VI with bilaterally barbed harpoons, parrot-beak chisels, and stemmed flint points, later known as Teyjat points.

Several portable art objects were also unearthed at this site. One very surprising piece was the radius bone of an eagle decorated with an engraving of a herd of reindeer.

These engravings form two distinct groups:

1- a semicircular composition beginning, at the base, with a right-facing horse. Above it, three aurochs (one male and two female) walk to the left. Near the top of the rock is a succession of deer, reindeer, horses, two bison and a bear, facing in different directions;

2- the second group again includes deer, this time with a reindeer lying down, a fawn, horses and a bear.

Forty-eight animals in all were counted at Teyjat including 5 unidentified deer species, 11 red deer, 13 reindeer, 10 horses, 3 aurochs, 4 bison, and 2 bears. The number of reindeer (more than one-quarter of the animals as a whole) is unusual in cave art.

The engravings are almost photographic in their realism. Some of the individual blocks of stone were set vertically into the archaeological layer dating from the Magdalenian V. It is therefore likely that the engravings date from this initial period of occupation. With the slightly more recent engravings in Limeuil, they have helped to define the main features of the artistic style that marked the end of the Magdalenian.

❐ The Pierre-Bourrinet museum near the cave provides a detailed approach to the cave as a whole and the artefacts found in the neighbouring Mège cave (Tel. +33 (0) 899 232 373).

**Photographic realism**
The end of the Magdalenian was marked by a very realistic style of drawing, as shown in this finely engraved drawing of a female auroch in Teyjat. The proportions and stance are very natural. Just behind the female is a male with its muzzle against her croup, suggesting that she is about to be mounted ■

**A porch dwelling in Rouffignac**
Mesolithic hunters occupied this cave entrance between 9,200 and 7,800 years ago. Digs have revealed superimposed hearths here, with bones from hunted animals and knapped flints, in particular geometric microliths from the Sauveterrian. The upper layers contained graves from the Neolithic and metal ages ■

**Graves in the Campniac cave**
Located in the Vieille-Cité valley, this cave was found to contain human bones, some of them charred, polished axes, cut flints, bone tools and pieces of jewellery (Late Neolithic). The human remains must have been those of the people who lived on the Ecorneboeuf Hill overlooking the valley ■

of seasonal resources. On the way, they also gathered roots, fruit, seeds and wild berries.

***Outdoor encampments*** were uncommon in Périgord. People lived in rock shelters or at cave mouths such as the Contie cave in Coulaures in the Isle basin and, more importantly, the cave at Rouffignac in the Vézère basin. They returned there for more than one thousand years, to camp, knap the flints that were dotted across the cave walls and light fires surrounded by stakes maybe used to hold roasting spits.

They left ***tiny flints*** characteristic of the Sauveterrian culture (named after Sauveterre-la-Lémance near Périgord). These microliths, pygmy triangles, sharpened bipoints (Sauveterrian points) and points with truncated bases (Rouffignac points) were made *in situ*, as is obvious from the microchisels also found here and the characteristic waste from knapping. Larger tools such as end-scrapers, and especially denticulates, could have been used for other activities like working wood. Some flint knives show a special gloss as if they had cut stems. However, it is unlikely that these stems came from cereal stalks, since wild cereals only grew in the Near East, and cereal crops were not planted in the West until later in the Neolithic. The inhabitants of Rouffignac probably harvested plants for bedding or basketry.

And what about dogs? Small wolves have been recorded immediately after the end of the period of glaciation, perhaps in the process of being domesticated if they had not been already. What is known for certain is that the last Mesolithic people in Rouffignac had dogs, almost 8,000 years ago.

## The first steps towards farming in the Early Stone Age

Some 7,000 years ago, a new lifestyle began to develop, having spread here from the Near East. The last hunters of the forest gradually became ***the first shepherds and farmers in Périgord***. The first signs appear a thousand years earlier with a change in the tools. Gradually, trapezes replace triangles. Transverse arrowheads, generally triangular with invasive retouching, were found in Rouffignac, Roc du Barbeau, and Peyrat near Saint-Rabier. In Rouffignac, the level dates from the middle of the 6th millennium, according to carbon 14

dating. These tiny arrowheads and the first associated microliths with invasive retouching are found throughout Southern France. They belonged to the first shepherds and farmers of the Stone Age.

***Efficient tools*** were needed to make clearings in the forest, turn over the fertile top soil, sow precious seeds, erect fencing, and harvest and store the grain. The polished axe became the basic tool of farmers who had previously used stone axes. Rich in flint and hard cobbles, Périgord was an excellent source of raw materials. The grey-greenish dolerite pebbles carried by the Auvézère from the Limousin, were rolled along by the Isle River and deposited just downstream from Périgueux, where they were turned into polished axes. Quarries have recently been discovered in the east of the *département* around Saint-Jean-de-Côle. In workshops that continued to operate for several thousand years, people made axes using the excellent flint from the Bergerac area as well as a range of other tools.

In the 5th millennium B.P., there were already sedentary farmer-stock breeders in Périgord.

**Polisher from Carves**
Knapped axe heads were polished by rubbing them for ten hours or more on blocks of sandstone, using an abrasive (e.g. sand) and a binder. The grooves in the polisher were used to polish the cutting edges of the axes while the shallower, oval indents were used to polish the flat surfaces and sides (Périgueux Museum) ■

**Vase from Campniac**
This is a flat-bottomed vase with lugs referred to as a "flowerpot". The clay is rough, containing plant debris, and the potting lacks skill. Along with the imperfect firing, these features are characteristic of the Late Neolithic era (Périgueux Museum) ■

**The Bonarme dolmen in Saint-Pardoux-et-Vielvic**
The megalith de Cayrelea, or "Lou Ped de la Vache", is still half buried within an earthen mound and covered with earth. The present entrance into the trapezoidal chamber is between the back stone and one of the kerbstones. The capstone is supported by two large parallel blocks forming a passage. This capstone bears two natural depressions which common people see as a cow's hoofprints ■

**The Blanc dolmen in Nojals-et-Clottes**
This dolmen, or Cros-de-la-Vuige, is often incorrectly referred to as a "passage grave". It stands on a mound probably built by people in the Neolithic Age. Its current condition does not correspond to the original construction. Today, the entrance is at the back of the building. The entrance "portico", which has collapsed, is typical of a style seen in the Angers area of France ■

## DOLMENS IN THE MIDDLE NEOLITHIC

Erect stone slabs delineate polygonal or rectangular chambers roofed by one or more large capstones. The chamber is preceded by a passage made of shorter vertical stone slabs or dry-stone walls originally covered by capstones. The construction was then covered by a mound of earth or, more often, rubble held in position by small internal walls, creating a cave-like appearance. Now these dolmens are no more than pathetic ruins.

Périgord has a large number of dolmens, some one hundred in all, but almost all of them were pillaged by treasure seekers in days gone by so nobody knows what they once contained, when they were built or, in many cases, what they originally looked like. They must have been erected and been in use over a period of at least a thousand years.

**Pottery from Campniac**
This round-bottomed vase dates from the Middle Neolithic, as do some of the sharp arrowheads, polished axes and jewellery found in the cave, which was also occupied in the Late or Final Mesolithic (Périgueux Museum) ■

***Their villages,*** set on spurs of rock or in valleys, have been destroyed by erosion, crops or alluvial soil. In the rock shelters and caves, the Neolithic levels were often destroyed in days gone by when digs were conducted into the Palaeolithic layers. This occurred in the famous sites in Les Eyzies such as Laugerie-Basse, Laugerie-Haute and La Mouthe to name but a few.

Yet ***burials*** from this period are known in Rouffignac or in the Skeleton shelter in Laugerie-Haute. In the second half of the 5th millennium B.P. strange monuments were erected in Périgord, built of rough or coarsely worked blocks of stone. These monuments were dolmens.

**Jewellery from Campniac**
This is a reconstitution using elements found separately in the cave e.g. pierced animal teeth, stone beads and a rough limestone pendant (Périgueux Museum) ■

## Settlement and collective cave burials in the Later Neolithic

In the 4th millennium B.C., Charente's Late Neolithic culture spread into the Dronne and Isle basins. The various groups still made pottery but of inferior quality. Flaked or polished stone tools were far more abundant. Other new implements include axe-hammers and polished stone double-axes which were time-consuming to make and fragile when finished.

Like their neighbours in Charente, the inhabitants of Dordogne adopted or developed causewayed settlements on high ground or even on the plains, building a single or multiple outer wall in a more or less circular layout. Aerial photography has revealed a few of them in the north of Périgord. Surveys in Bouteilles-Saint-Sébastien and Festalemps have revealed traces of the Matignon culture. The moats, dug with antler or flint picks, may have provided the building materials for the walls and, possibly, for houses, but they have been destroyed by erosion and centuries of ploughing. It is unclear why people built similar moated settlements in sandy or rocky soils as they did in the Isle Valley (Fontaine de la Demoiselle in Saint-Léon-sur-l'Isle).

***Collective burials,*** sometimes with several dozen skeletons, were uncovered in caves in the Isle Basin (Campniac, next to Périgueux) and Dordogne Basin (Eybral). Often the bones had been removed, reordered and even partially cremated. The grave goods were often poor and included an occasional polished axe, rough pottery, perforated animal teeth, limestone beads, disks with two holes made from bone or mother of pearl from fresh water mussels. The same peoples must have reused or even built the dolmens. The gallery graves in the southern Périgord (Marsalès) may date from this period. This "Isle-Dordogne group" bears a close resemblance to the Seine-Oise-Marne group from the Late Neolithic in the Paris Basin.

Thanks to these bones, we know more about the ***physical appearance of the people of Perigord at that time***. In many ways, they resembled their ancestors: there were few immigrants to change the basic characteristics of the people. Their skulls were elongated, sometimes carinated, and their faces were fairly broad, but they were probably generally less robust than Upper Palaeolithic populations. Changes in living conditions may account for a great deal. The selection pressures which were still quite high in the Upper Palaeolithic decreased gradually in the Neolithic. A drop in the meat content of the diet and increased protection against the elements and other dangers, also meant a far healthier environment for the sick, the elderly, and children. The ensuing gracilisation is clearly visible. This process is equivalent to the skeletal reductions observed in domesticated animals compared to their wild ancestors. Humans are self-domesticated animals.

**Fontaine de la Demoiselle (Saint-Léon-sur-l'Isle)**
This site was occupied in the Late Neolithic (white sand with coloured strips) and in the Final Mesolithic (reddish-brown sand) (digs by J. Roussot-Larroque)

**Eybral Cave in Le Cous-et-Bigaroque**
The cave contained the scattered bones of almost 80 skeletons of adults and children, some of them charred. Some of the skulls, like the one on the right, were trepanned for reasons unknown (reconstitution at the Aquitaine Museum, Bordeaux)

**Flint dagger from Saint-Seurin-de-Prats**
The retouching, done after polishing, is particularly fine. These beautiful daggers tended to be objects of prestige for which pieces of flint were sometimes imported from Le Grand-Pressigny (Indre-et-Loire)

# The first metal workers

*Early in the 3rd millennium B.C., flint knapping produced arrows with wings and peduncles, and large retouched blades or "daggers", some of them twenty centimetres in length.*

### Changes during the Later Neolithic

In the Bergerac area, flint blades were imported from Le Grand-Pressigny (Touraine) or copied. They were made from so-called "pounds of butter". The Artenacian culture spread to Périgord from Normandy. Its fine ceramics had incised or pontillated decoration and the handles were shaped like birds' beaks (or were nose-shaped).

***Settlements*** were built on promontories, in valleys and even on riverbanks. The Artenacians dug ditches, built earth and stone dikes, colonised the land and built houses of wattle and daub with thatched roofs.

They buried their dead in caves and rock shelters, as well as dolmens. Not all of the dolmens were new. Some were older and reused. Often smaller and simpler than in the Middle Neolithic, they were quite numerous particularly in the Isle basin (Saint-Aquilin) and in southern Périgord (Saint-Pardoux-et-Vielvic).

The last Neolithic men used ***gold and copper.*** Metalworking first appeared in the Near East before spreading to the southern rim of the ore-rich Massif Central, the Limousin area and the Pyrenees. Towards the middle of the 3rd millennium B.C., people used copper daggers and axes in Périgord. Flat copper axes similar to the earlier polished stone axes were discovered singly (Boulazac) or in small groups of two or three (Saint-Capraise-d'Eymet, Saint-Martial-d'Artenset). Copper daggers were found in the Fontanguillère cave south of Bergerac. The flat daggers were commonly used throughout Europe and were closely associated with bell-beakers decorated with patches or parallel horizontal lines, using a cord or comb.

**Bronze dagger blade from Le Coux-et-Bigaroque**
Its engraved decoration was inspired by the civilisation living in the Rhône corridor during the Early Bronze Age ■

**The oldest examples of metalworking**
A copper dagger with a tongue, found in the underground stream in Fontanguillère (Rouffignac-de-Sigoules). It is very simple in shape, suggestive of the Campaniform civilisation. Flat copper axe from Manzac-sur-Vern: the earliest metal axes were shaped like the earlier stone axes (Périgueux Museum) ■

## The arrival of the Early Bronze age and the first "princes" of Périgord

Adding tin to copper was found to improve its qualities – and ***bronze was invented.*** Originally, metalworkers used a natural tin oxide, cassiteite, panned in rivers (in Brittany, Spain and the Monts de Blond in Limousin). Gradually the tin content rose to 10% or more. Innovations began in the Massif Central and spread along the valleys into Périgord. The first low-flanged axes derived from the flat axes were found in Saint-Méard-de-Dronne.

In Port-Sainte-Foy, ***dredging*** of the Dordogne produced several thin low-tin bronze daggers with rivet holes and a ring-headed pin similar to Swiss and Italian types. A dagger blade from Coux-et-Bigaroque bears a pattern of engraved lines and dots, similar to examples from the Rhone Valley. The sword from the Singleyrac tomb near Bergerac may have been produced by the same culture. The hollow bronze hilt of this 40 centimetre-long sword was probably cast using the lost wax process and riveted to the blade. The stone coffin and its grave goods (thirteen gold spirals, a gold ring, a gold rod, and an axe) have now disappeared but they suggested the existence of an elite in Périgord in the days of the "princes" of the Early Bronze Age in Armorica, Wessex, or Saxony.

Human bones and the skeletal remains of a horse were said to have accompanied a beautiful sword with a bronze handle found in the Lizonne Marshes. It is 84 centimetres long and has a bronze handle riveted onto the blade, a mushroom-shaped pommel, a trifoliate hilt and thin incised fan-shaped decoration on the blade. It is a masterpiece, comparable to a handful of other similar items found throughout France. The gold spiral from Le Grand Roc in Les Eyzies dates from the Early or Middle Bronze Age although it was discovered in a much later location. Other burials were more modest. The skeleton found in a narrow, downward sloping gallery in Les Partisans cave in Marquay, was buried with only a few pots.

**The gold spiral from Laugerie-Basse**
Consisting of a long gold rod with pointed ends rolled into a spiral, it was discovered in the cleft of a rock in Le Grand Roc near Laugerie-Basse in Les Eyzies and was almost impossible to reach. It dates from the Early or Middle Bronze Age (Les Eyzies Museum) ■

## Prosperity in the Middle Bronze Age

As early as the 15th century B.C., increasing numbers of bronze objects were cast, hammered into shape, and decorated with incised ornamentation. Axes, daggers, swords, or bracelets were very rare in settlements. They were mainly discovered in hoards, ritual deposits, private treasures, or foundry stocks throughout the region from the Ribérac area (La Rochebeaucourt-et-Argentine et Vanxains) to the basins of the rivers Isle (Coulaures, Saint-Front-de-Pradoux, Mussidan), Auvézère (Hautefort), Vézère (Thonac, Fleurac, Meyrals) and Dordogne (Berbiguières) and on down to the south of Périgord (Issigeac) etc.

As in nearby Gironde, flanged axes were the commonest find. Local forms like the Thonac axe with a narrow edge, a wide cutting sur-

**A bronze sword from Saint-Paul-Lizonne**
This magnificent bronze-handled sword 84 cm in length was discovered near the Lizonne Marshes, with the bones of a horse. The sword is of a very rare type from the Middle Bronze Age also found in the Massif central and Languedoc regions (Périgueux Museum) ■

face, and concave sides, were also found in Rouffignac and Vanxains. Some of the axes are decorated with a hammered imbricated V-shaped pattern. The axes are all from the same moulds and were therefore made by local, possibly itinerant, bronzesmiths. As for palstaves, different types existed side by side, some resembling the types from the Atlantic coast or Massif Central. Both types may be found in the same hoard (Hautefort, Fleurac).

Middle Bronze Age ***bracelets*** are massive open bangles with slightly thicker ends and geometric decoration e.g. ladders, chevrons and hatched triangles. Some hoards contain only bracelets (La Rochebeaucourt-et-Argentine, La Calévie cave in Meyrals); others may have contained axes and bracelets (Fleurac). A single bangle was found at Gorge d'Enfer in Les Eyzies. Some bracelets were designed to be worn together: the four found in La Calévie formed a composite piece of jewellery weighing 427 grams. Typical of the time was decoration consisting of panels separated by vertical lines (Les Eyzies, Meyrals, Fleurac), a style that was commonplace throughout the west and south west of France. The Dordogne was the fashion centre of its day.

Little is known about ***the housing***. Not far from Port-Sainte-Foy, Médoc-style pottery decorated with cords and pastillages is very common, as it is in the centre and south of western France. This style of pottery spread inland, at least as far as the area around Les Eyzies.

The Font-de-Gaume cave near Les Eyzies produced a bone arrow with wings and peduncle (cf. La Roque-Saint-Christophe), a beautiful bronze pin with a wider, perforated neck and engraved decoration, a beaker with handle and a polypod vase. The pin, which is typical of the Barrow

**Middle Bronze Age bracelets from La Calévie cave (Meyrals)**
These four engraved bracelets were discovered by the Spéléo-Club de Périgueux. Each bracelet has a larger diameter than the previous one so that they fit snugly on the forearm. The largest and smallest have the same decoration consisting of cross-hatched triangles (Périgueux Museum) ■

**Close-up of a bronze bracelet from La Calévie**
On the two central bracelets in the set, the panels are separated by vertical bands, a typical feature of Middle Bronze Age decoration in the region ■

culture, is similar to bronzework discovered on the left bank of the Rhine. Why this hoard in this deep cave? Other caves including Rouffignac were explored but did not provide an answer. The walls of one of them were decorated (Les Fraux in Saint-Martin-de-Fressengeas).

In the Sarlat area, a few cliff-dwellings were discovered at Roc de Saint-Augustin in Carsac. The systems of small walls on the top of some of the region's hills may have been built over older constructions dating from this period. The excavation at La Roque-Saint-Christophe established that animal husbandry was practised and that pork was the meat of choice in Périgord cooking. The hunting of red deer, roe-deer, and boar, in addition to fishing, added variety to the standard diet.

In Southern Périgord and neighbouring Quercy, bronze seems to be even more unusual in dwellings but ***pottery*** was commonplace. There were vases with multiple feet,

**Bronze axe hoard in Vanxains**
The axes had been deposited in a hole in the ground (Archaeological Park in Beynac). Another hoard, in Thonac, contained 27 unpolished cast axes, apparently all made using the same foundry die ■

**A farmer's flint scythe**
This blade from the Vaufrey cave (in Cénac) is made of pale golden flint that, without any doubt, has been imported. It has a characteristic sheen. It was used to cut the stalks of cereal crops or reeds some 5,000 years ago ■

## DREDGING THE DORDOGNE

- Weapons, which are rare in the hoards in Périgords, have been found by dredging the River Dordogne. Trapezoidal-hilted daggers are not infrequent, with two or often four rivets. One was found in Fleix and four in Port-Sainte-Foy, where a sword with a two-rivet hilt and wide blade was also discovered. The weapons are obviously related to the Middle Bronze Tumulus culture of south-west Germany and Alsace, as well as the Massif Central, central-western France and the Gironde.
- Magnificent socketed spearheads have also been recovered from the Dordogne River. These include a 43.5 cm long, Sucy-en-Brie type spearhead from Le Fleix, and some spearheads with pontillated decoration and incised lines from Port-Sainte-Foy. Two of them are basal-looped, a British style imitated in France. Some of them still had part of their wooden haft in their sockets.

**The ford across the Vézère**
Before the days of modern roads, travellers had to use fords to cross rivers and many of them have revealed bronze artefacts that were either lost or thrown into the water as an offering ■

cups and jugs, exuberant decoration consisting of engravings, incisions and points (but rarely stamping). In the cliff-dwellings of Le Comte, at the confluence of the Céou and the Dordogne Rivers, vases of this type, decorated with herring bone or hatched triangle motifs, were found. Human bones and even a child's burial were uncovered there.

### The heyday of bronze in Périgord

The great trends which marked the start of the Late Bronze Age reached the Périgord region, which, for the next three centuries, was strongly influenced by the so-called "Urnfield culture". ***Pottery*** achieved a higher quality. It was finer and more delicate, shiny black or light beige in colour. The shapes were influenced by artefacts made of sheet bronze. The rills and parallel geometric lines acquired subtle nuances in light and shade. Large platters were decorated with foliage or stars.

This pottery quickly became popular throughout much of France (from the east to the central west and south). Here, it is made on site. In La Roque-Saint-Christophe, the clay contains calcite; it comes from the caves higher up the cliffs. Grinding stones were found in some of the occupation layers. They had been used to crush heated quartz cobbles into a fine powder which was then used as a degreaser. No doubt there were pottery kilns nearby. Some of the most beautiful vases were inlaid with strips of tin (Reignac in Tursac). People even made pottery bracelets, some of them decorated, imitating lignite rings.

Like La Roque-Saint-Christophe, many of ***the rock shelters*** were reoccupied at this time (Reignac, Laugerie-Basse). There were also ***deep caves*** (Rouffignac, La Martine in Domme), inhospitable underground streams (the Fontanguillère) or caves high up in rock walls and difficult to reach (the "Church" cave in Guilhem in Les Eyzies).

***Agriculture*** was a thriving industry that made use of grinding stones and large cordoned urns as granaries. Evidence of the farming of cattle, goats and pigs has been found. People still hunted. In La Roque-Saint-Christophe, one of the trophies, a curved boar tusk, was 18 cm long, and a perforated bone arrowpoint is believed to have been used to hunt birds.

***Few graves*** have been found. Two skeletons were discovered, lying head to foot in La Roque-Saint-Christophe. Many bones were removed from the underground river in La Fontanguillère where it is thought that the bodies were laid out on slatted platforms supported by wooden stakes. In the deep recesses of Rouffignac, pottery deposits were sometimes accompanied by a handful of ashes. The Maurélie cave in Plazac contained complete vessels, a pin and a bronze bracelet but there were only a couple of human bones nearby. This suggests some mysterious ritual.

**Disc-headed pin and a spear tip**
Discovered in 1889 near l'Hermitage and the source of the River Toulon (Périgueuc), these two bronze artefacts are both beautifully decorated. They come from a relatively early period in the Final Bronze Age

***Metal*** is often rare in these sites except for small objects like the knife, arrowhead and pins from La Roque-Saint-Christophe and the pin from Laugerie-Basse. Items must have

## ☛ LA ROQUE SAINT-CHRISTOPHE

One of the most picturesque settlement sites on the Vézère occupied the lower rock shelters at the foot of the great cliff in La Roque-Saint-Christophe (Peyzac-le-Moustier), close to a ford. Backing onto the rock and rockfalls were lightly-built constructions supported by wooden posts, of which a few traces have been found. The layout suggests the existence of a small circular building, possibly a house. The pottery was made on site and consisted of large fat urns, jugs with smooth or braided cord decoration, finer cups (some of them burnished) with incised or stamped patterns and polypod vases (with small feet). One level C14-dated to 3,040+/–120 B.P. (or about 1,430 to 1,120 B.C.) yielded some vases with decorative triangles, diamonds or squares that were either stamped (using a wood or bone die) or excised (by removing some of the clay). The designs then received white inlay. This pottery style reveals some of the same continental influences of the Tumulus culture which were already visible in the production of metal objects such as the swords and daggers with trapezoid hilts dredged from the Dordogne. Layers of ash containing bronze prills and pieces of slag suggest that bronzesmithing existed here. A bronze flanged axe (a miniature reproduction of the Thonac axes) was discovered in the nearby Combe de Banne.

Some 1,300 years B.C. in La Roque-Saint-Christophe, styles changed. The

**La Roque-Saint-Christophe**
The rock shelters on the banks of the Vézère were occupied in the Gravettian, Neolithic and Bronze Ages. In fact, some of them continued to be occupied until the Middle Ages. Set into the cliff was a mediaeval village that was inhabited until the French Revolution ■

**Middle Bronze Age jug from La Roque-Saint-Christophe**
Its decoration of stamped and excised triangles was inspired by the Tumulus culture in the east of France. The indentations were designed to be filled with inlays of white matter (digs by J. Roussot-Larroque) ■

**La Roque-Saint-Christophe shelter**
At the foot of the impressive cliff, the stratified layers of the Middle and Final Bronze Ages are of great significance in improving our knowledge of these periods in Périgord (digs by J. Roussot-Larroque) ■

cups and bowls were carinated with everted edges, decorated with shallow horizonal and vertical lines or with rilled wart or backle decoration as in Yonne or in the regions to the west of the Alps. This style appears to replace stamping or carving. The same inspiration is observed in metal objects such as the median winged axe from Villars, the disk-headed pin from Le Toulon in Périgueux (found with an impressively decorated spearhead), and the Rixheim sword dredged from the Dordogne River at Port-Sainte-Foy. A superb bronze-hilted sword, also dredged from the Dordogne River in the same area, is a rare type dating from a slightly later period.

The rock shelters low down the cliff at La Roque-Saint-Christophe (visible from the road) were occupied again and again during the Bronze Age.

❒ Tel. +33 (0) 553 507 045.

been melted down again and redesigned to suit current trends. Only a few isolated artefacts have been found, rare funeral objects, items that have been dredged up and the small hoard in Saint-Front-de-Pradoux (two complete axes with subterminal wings and ring, and fragments of four others, with heel, ring and round socket, of a type also found in Gironde). Other isolated finds include continental items such as the winged axe of Les Eyzies, with a constriction below the wing not so different from the Swiss type associated with "Rhine-Swiss-Eastern-France" pottery. The same influences may be seen in ornaments such as pins, belt buckles or chest plates, pendants, and small bracelets at Fontanguillère.

Influences from the west, however, are seen in three pistilliform Atlantic swords (from sites near Périgueux, Saint-Cyprien and La Fontanguillère). The region served as a link between bronzemakers on the Atlantic coast and inland (Limousin and Auvergne), where similar swords trace a route back to the Saône Valley and Switzerland.

## The end of the Bronze Age in Périgord

The late stage of the Bronze Age (from 900 to 800 B.C.) was a continuation of the preceeding period. The same ***settlement sites*** were continuously occupied and even some higher sites were re-occupied.

***Ceramics*** were still of the same high quality that characterised the previous phase but the shapes were simpler and softer. A typical vase of this period is the "onion bulb" beaker, with oblique rim, a globular body, and a narrow base, which became widespread in Périgord, in the valleys of the Dordogne (Casteval in Urval, La Roque-Saint-Christophe, Laugerie-Basse and Puypinsou in the Isle Valley). Meanders that had appeared slightly earlier now decorated rimless cups and bowls. The interior of dishes was decorated with concentric rilling or stamped panels alternating with undecorated areas. A carmine red made from hematite was used to decorate some vases. The most beautiful vessels were decorated with black and red concentric circles.

***Bronze*** was still being smelted (slag and buningot in Laugerie-Basse) but there were few metal objects in houses. Nor were there many hoards. A few isolated finds including a carps' tongue sword at Saint-Léon-sur-l'Isle and small earrings in gold-plated bronze from Fontanguillère were evidence of contact with the Atlantic area. A magnificent bronze roasting spit for ritual feasts was dredged up in the Dordogne near Port-Sainte-Foy.

***Burials*** were just as rare as they were in earlier times. Beneath the entrance to Rouffignac cave, a burned area repeatedly dug out and paved with stones, and containing fragments of human bones, is believed to have been a funeral pyre. A dig has also uncovered a bronze button with a "bow tie" shank dating from the Late Bronze Age. In a gallery deep inside the cave, a (ritual ?) deposit contained dome-shaped buttons, resembling the brass buttons of a uniform and a bronze spearhead. Similar buttons, with rings, were found in a deposit in La Croix in Terrasson.

## New beginnings : the Early Iron Age in Périgord

From the 8th century B.C., iron began to compete with bronze. A good example of this technological transition is the iron-bladed sword with a bronze hilt dredged from the Dordogne at Port-Sainte-Foy. Bronze and iron swords were equally used for a short time but iron quickly became the metal of choice. Périgord had extensive surface iron ore deposits and the ore could be smelted using what

**Pedestal urn from Jumilhac-le-Grand**
This urn containing charred human bones comes from a barrow at La Lande de Prunou in Jumilhac-le-Grand. The geometric pattern painted with graphite is typical of the Early Iron Age in eastern Périgord, Limousin and Charente (Périgueux Museum)

were still rudimentary methods. The new technology, from the Eastern Mediterranean, gradually spread through Central Europe and the Balkans before reaching Western Europe, possibly brought here by horsemen who left behind a trail of barrows skirting the south side of the Massif Central and continuing up into Périgord. Certain regional peculiarities distinguish these populations from the ***Early Iron Age***; they were deeply rooted by the end of the Late Bronze Age.

However, around the 7th or 6th century B.C., settlements that had been continuously occupied since the Bronze Age, were abandoned. From then on, people preferred to live on hilltops (Écornebœuf near Périgueux). They were easier to defend and they took people up out of valleys that had become damp as a result of climate change *circa* 800 B.C. Walls were built and moats were sometimes dug out of the rock.

***Graves*** took the form of barrows, mounds of earth that were sometimes heaped over a stone core protecting a central chamber (Les Landes de Prunou in Jumilhac-le-Grand), possibly with a circle of stones on the periphery, although this was commoner in Limousin. The deceased were cremated on a funeral pyre. The charred bones were collected up, sometimes washed, then placed in a pottery urn, occasionally accompanied by additional vases and a few metallic objects, weapons or jewellery. The barrow could be built directly over the pyre.

The pottery was very fine and elegant in form with high "skittle" necks (Jumilhac-le-Grand) and, in some cases, supported by a tall hollow stand. Decoration was done with graphite (mined in Limousin). Complex, silver-gray, geometric patterns appear against a brown background. The inspiration for this technique must have come from Central Europe. Such luxury pottery has also been found in settlement sites (Écornebœuf).

Some of the deceased obviously had high social status, like the person buried under the great Tuckey Barrow in Lanouaille. This impressive barrow (over 25 metres in diameter and almost 4 metres high), contained four graphite vases, the deeply decayed remains of a bronze vessel with suspended rings, and a magnificent earring made of electrum – an alloy of gold and silver. The design for this unique filigree earring, decorated with soldered gold beads, was inspired by Mediterranean goldsmiths – possibly Etruscans. The bronze vase may also come from the Mediterranean. Thus, as early as the sixth century B.C., there existed a wealthy élite in Périgord and they were in more or less direct contact with the cultural centres of Central Europe and the Mediterranean.

## The real face of Périgord

Over the centuries and millennia of prehistory and protohistory, Périgord gained its own character. From flaked pebbles to decorated caves, from stone to bronze, and then to iron, the entire region has gradually developed its own unique personality.

After the magnificent accomplishment of the prehistoric "Sistine Chapel", Périgord did not fall back into obscurity, as one might have thought. Its place in more recent prehistory and protohistory, all too often ignored, foreshadowed the important role this region was later to play in pre-Roman Gaul.

**A rock shelter near La Madeleine**
On the banks of the Vézère, the alternating periods of freezing and thaws that continued year after year eroded the softest layers of the cliff, eventually creating a rock shelter. It was an ideal place to live. However, people in the Palaeolithic also built their houses in the open air, as we now know thanks to the major work that has uncovered their encampments

**The Richard Cave in Les Eyzies**
Palaeolithic people are sometimes referred to as "cave men" but it's a long-standing myth. They never lived in the depths of caves, only at the cave mouths on a few occasions. Sometimes they explored deep underground, drawing and creating veritable underground sanctuaries. Their motives were probably religious in nature rather than related to magic, shamans or totems but this did not preclude an undoubted love of the aesthetic

## Around the hearth in the rock shelter

The hearth, inside a dwelling or at its entrance, is a vital feature. A small fire is very effective in a hut or a rock shelter. The fire provides light and heat. It lengthens the days and prolongs summer. It sterilises, reduces and transforms meat and plant-based foods. It makes flint easier to work with and hardens the tips of spears. And it is while sitting round the fire that people tell stories and legends, gradually giving rise to social interaction (shooting a film about the Pataud shelter) ■

0
10 km
Limoges
Angoulême
HAUTE-VIENNE
87
CHARENTE
16
CORRÈZE
19
CHAR.-MAR.
17
GIRONDE
33
47
LOT-ET-GARONNE
LOT
46
Brive-la-Gaillarde
Cahors
Charente
Vienne
Tardoire
Dronne
Isle
Auvézère
Vézère
Dordogne
Lot
N 10
N 141
N 21
N 89
A 89
A 20
A 62
N 20
D 704
D 85
D 939
D 708
D 674
D 705
D 710
D 660
D 936
D 933
D 104
D 60
D 911
Teyjat
Nontron
Mareuil
Roc Plat
Villars
Thiviers
Lanouaille
Vendoire
Paussac
Brantôme
Verteillac
Rochereil
Le Fourneau du Diable
Excideuil
Coulaures
Pont-d'Ambon
Ribérac
Raymonden
Goudaud
Dépôts de Vanxains
St-Aquilin
Périgueux
Badegoule
La Croix
Ecornebœuf
Campniac
Thenon
La Roche-Chalais
Chavagnac
La Fontaine-de la Demoiselle
Montignac
Vergt
Mussidan
Montpon-Ménestérol
Les Eyzies-de-Tayac-Sireuil
Sarlat-la-Canédat
Port-Ste-Foy
Bergerac
Gare de Couze
Lalinde
Limeuil
St-Chamassy
Pech de l'Azé
Eybral
Beynac-et-Cazenac
La Gravette
Les Plaguettes
La Fontanguillère
Cussac
Cayre Leva
Le Comte
Domme
Combe Grenal
Les Jean-Blancs
Peyre-Nègre
Bonarme
Singleyrac
Le Blanc
Marsalès
La Courrège
Monpazier
Vergt de Biron
Villefranche-du-Périgord
Dordogne
Rock shelter
Cave
Megalith
Outdoor site or isolated find
Museum

**Périgord, the Land of Prehistory**

Périgord, now the *département* of Dordogne, was nicknamed the "Land of Mankind" a few years ago. Of course, it is not the birthplace of prehistoric man, nor even his cradle. *Homo habilis* appeared in Africa 2.5 million years ago. Périgord, though, is the land of Neanderthal and Cro-Magnon Man.

Most of the major sites lie in the valleys at the foot of the cliffs. However, that does not mean that prehistoric man did not also live, as we do, in the open, protected by the simple roof of his hide-covered hut. Here, though, Man preferred the rock shelters that provided a ready-made roof and that were situated not far from areas through which game would migrate. The first prehistorians, beginning with E. Lartet and H. Christy in 1863, focussed their interest on these rock shelters, which were much easier to locate than outdoor settlements

Close to the "Land of Mankind" are prehistoric sites that tend to be forgotten, lying in the shadow of Périgord's more famous sites. Among them are the small cave in Pair-non-Pair in the lower Dordogne Valley north of Libourne (numerous Aurignacian engravings), the Solutrean site at Roc-de-Sers on the edge of Périgord near Angoulême which provided some superb low reliefs (now in the National Archaeology Museum in Saint-Germain-en-Laye), and the cave-sanctuaries in Cougnac and Pech-Merle in Quercy south-east of Sarlat. A large number of decorated stone or bone artefacts are now kept in museums elsewhere (especially the National Archaeology Museum and the Aquitaine Museum in Bordeaux). A visit of these places and museums is a wonderful way to round off a great trip through Périgord ■

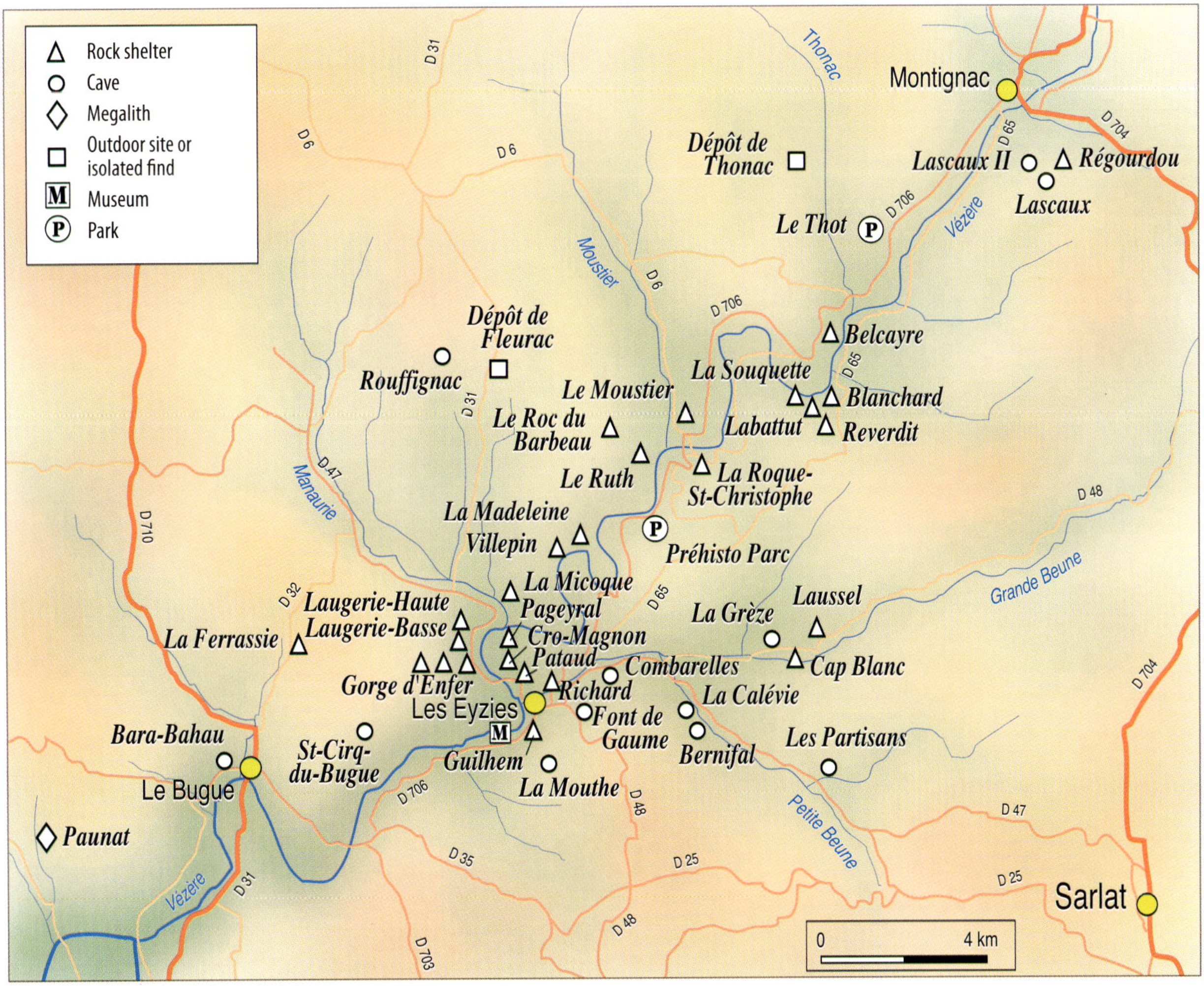

# Cultural sites
## (other than caves and prehistoric rock shelters)

**Beynac · Archaeological park** The everyday life of farmers and metalworkers from the Stone Age to the days of the Ancient Gauls. Tel. +33 (0) 553 29 50 40.

**Bordeaux · Musée d'Aquitaine** Bas-reliefs of human figures from Laussel. Sculpted bison from Cap Blanc. Large series of collections from sites in Périgord. Tel. 05 56 01 51 00.

The Prehistoparc in Tursac: one of the scenes from prehistory. Men hunting a mammoth trapped in a pit ■

The International Prehistory Centre ("PIP") in Les Eyzies, whose resolutely modern architecture forms a beautiful contrast to the cliff above it, is very attractively laid out ■

**Brantôme · Musée Fernand-Desmoulin** Prehistoric collection of industries and art objects from Rochereil. Tel. +33 (0) 553 05 80 63.

**Les Eyzies-de-Tayac · Musée national de Préhistoire** The national museum of prehistory reflects contemporary archaeological research and is the *in situ* emanation of the exceptionally rich prehistoric past of the "open-air museum" that is the Vézère Valley, with its plethora of prehistoric settlements and cave-sanctuaries, some of which have been placed on Unesco's World Heritage list. Its unique collections (6 million artefacts of which 18,000 are on display) make it a global benchmark for the last four hundred millenia. They fill 1,500 sq. metres of museum in a brand new building inaugurated in 2004. Items from the collections from the national archaeology museum in Saint-Germain-en-Laye near Paris were recently brought to the museum in Les Eyzies for display, in particular decorated tools from La Madeleine and a pink sandstone lamp from Lascaux. Prehistoric collections from Périgord can also be seen in other French and foreign museums. Tel. +33 (0) 553 064 545.

**Les Eyzies-de-Tayac · Pôle international de Préhistoire** Visitors centre. Tel. +33 (0) 553 069 281.

**Les Eyzies-de-Tayac · Roc de Cazelle** A life-sized re-

The National Prehistory Museum in Les Eyzies-de-Tayac

construction of the daily life of cave dwellers from prehistoric times to the present day. Tel. +33 (0) 553 594 609.

**London • British Museum** Christy Collection, part of the artefacts found by Lartet and Christy in 1863-1864: tools and works of art from caves in Les Eyzies, Gorge d'Enfer, Laugerie-Basse and La Madeleine. Reverdit Collection: decorated bone ring from La Tuillière in Saint-Léon-sur-Vézère. Tel. +44 (0)20 7323 8299.

**Montignac • Lascaux II** See boxed text, page 47. Tel. +33 (0) 553 056 565 (Sémitour).

**Périgueux • Musée d'Art et d'Archéologie du Périgord** Portable art (notably from Raymonden), and Aurignacian paintings and engravings on stone blocks. Human skeletons from Régourdou (Mousterian) and Raymonden (Magdalenian). Stone Age and BronzeAge collections. Tel. +33 (0) 553 064 070.

**Saint-Germain-en-Laye • Musée de l'Archéologie nationale** Items from the most significant sites in Périgord. Tel. +33 (0) 139 101 300.

**Thonac • Le Thot** See boxed text, page 47. Tel. +33 (0) 553 056 565 (Sémitour).

**Tursac • Préhistoparc** Life-sized tableaux showing the everyday life of Neandertal and Cro-Magnon hunter-gatherers. Tel. +33 (0) 553 507 319.

# A few books

*L'art des cavernes. Atlas des grottes ornées paléolithiques françaises.* Ministère de la Culture, Imprimerie nationale, Paris, 1984 (collective work).

Aujoulat (N.). *Lascaux, le geste, l'espace et le temps*, Seuil, Paris, 2004.

Blanchet (J.-Cl.) and Cleyet-Merle (J.-J.). *Les Eyzies-de-Tayac et la vallée de la Vézère*. Coll. "Itinéraires", Éditions du Patrimoine, 2007.

Bordes (F.). *Leçons sur le Paléolithique*. Coll. "CNRS Plus", Presses du CNRS, 2 vols., Paris, 1992.

Breuil (H.). *Quatre cents siècles d'art pariétal*. Centre d'études et de documentation préhistoriques, Montignac, 1952.

Chevillot (Chr.). *Sites et cultures de l'âge de bronze en Périgord*. Éditions Vesunna, Périgueux, 1989.

Cleyet-Merle (J.-J.). *La province préhistorique des Eyzies. 400 000 ans d'implantation humaine*. CNRS Éditions, Paris, 2001.

Cleyet-Merle (J.-J.). *Musée national de Préhistoire des Eyzies, album*. Meeting of national museums, 2007.

Delluc (B. et G.). *Visiter l'abri Pataud*. Éditions Sud Ouest, Bordeaux, 1998.

Delluc (B. et G.). *Connaître Lascaux*. Éditions Sud Ouest, Bordeaux, 2006 (photographs by Ray Delvert).

Delluc (B. et G.). *L'art pariétal archaïque en Aquitaine*. Éditions du CNRS, Paris, 1991 (XXVIII[e] supplément à *Gallia Préhistoire*).

Delluc (B. et G.). *Dictionnaire de Lascaux*. Éditions Sud Ouest, Bordeaux, 2008.

Delporte (H.). *L'image des animaux dans l'art préhistorique*. Picard, Paris, 1990.

Delporte (H.). *L'image de la femme dans l'art préhistorique*. Picard, Paris, 1993.

Leroi-Gourhan (A.). *Préhistoire de l'art occidental*. Citadelles et Mazenod, Paris, 1995 (new edition reviewed and extended by B. and G. Delluc).

Lorblanchet (M.). *Les grottes ornées de la préhistoire. Nouveaux regards*. Éditions Errance, Paris, 1995.

Lorblanchet (M.). *La naissance de l'art. Genèse de l'art préhistorique*. Éditions Errance, Paris, 1999.

Plassard (M.-O. et J.). *La grotte de Rouffignac*. Éditions Sud Ouest, Bordeaux, 1989.

Plassard (J.). *Le sanctuaire des mammouths*. Seuil, Paris, 1999.

Roussot (A.). *Visiter le Cap Blanc*. Éditions Sud Ouest, Bordeaux, 1994.

Roussot (A.). *Visiter les abris de Laugerie-Basse*. Éditions Sud Ouest, Bordeaux, 1996.

Roussot (A.). *L'art préhistorique*. Éditions Sud Ouest, Bordeaux, 1997 (new updated edition).

Roussot (A.). *Petit glossaire de l'art préhistorique au Paléolithique*. Éditions Confluences, Bordeaux, 1998.

Roussot (A.). *La Vénus à la corne et Laussel*. Coll. "Les chefs-d'œuvre du musée d'Aquitaine", Éditions Sud Ouest, Bordeaux, 2000.

Vialou (D.) (sous la dir. de). *La Préhistoire. Histoire et Dictionnaire*. Coll. "Bouquins", Robert Laffont, Paris, 2004.

White (R.). *Préhistoire*. Éditions Sud Ouest, Bordeaux, 1993.

# Index



# Iconography

**Drawings**

J. Allain: p. 47 (bottom left).
A. Bonnamy: p. 5 (bottom).
B. and G. Delluc: p. 45 (top).
M. Féaux (coll. SHAP): p. 26 (top).
E. Guerrier: p. 9.
D. Peyrony: p. 22.
S. Rossy-Delluc: p. 34 (bottom).
A. Roussot: p. 90, 93 (top).

**Photo credits**

P. Bardou: p. 41 (top), 95 (top).
P. Bardou-A. Roussot: p. 64.
A. Bordes : p. 116 left, 117.
C. Chevillot: p. 103 (middle).
B. and G. Delluc: p. 7, 10-11, 12, 14, 21 (top), 23, 24-25, 27 (bottom), 28, 29, 30, 31, 32-33, 34 (middle), 39 (top), 39 (bottom right), 40, 42 (top), 44, 47 (middle and bottom right), 59, 6, 60-61, 62, 63, 65 (bottom), 68, 70 (top), 71 (bottom), 72, 73, 74, 75, 76, 84, 85 (bottom), 92 (left), 94 (right), 96-97, 99 (middle), 103 (top), 111, 112-113
H. Delporte (coll.): p. 34 (top).
R. Delvert: p. 1 (left), 47 (top), 48, 49, 50-51, 52-53, 54-55, 56-57.
G. de Fayolle: p. 13 (top).
A. Glory (coll. MNHN): p. 4, 46 (top),
A. Glory (coll. Delluc): p. 45.
G. Lalanne (coll.): p. 9.
J. Lagrange: p. 15 (bottom), 45 (bottom),
A. Leroi-Gourhan (coll. Delluc): p. 65 (top), 82, 83, 91.
H. Movius (coll.): p. 15 (top right).
Musée des Eyzies: p. 93 (bottom).
B. Pierret: p. 15 (top, left).
J. Plassard: p. 1 (middle), 86-87, 88, 94 (left).
A. Roussot: p. 1 (right), 5 (top), 8, 16, 17, 18, 19, 20, 21 (bottom), 24, 27, 35, 36, 37, 38, 39 (bottom left), 42 (bottom), 43, 46 (middle and bottom), 58, 66, 67, 69, 70 (bottom), 71 (top), 77, 80, 81, 90, 93 (top), 93, 95 (bottom), 97, 98, 99 (bottom), 100, 101, 102, 104, 105, & 06, 107, 109.
J. Roussot-Larroque: p. 99 (top), 103 (bottom).
D. Vialou: p. 78.
J. Vertut: p. 85 top.

**In front cover:** photo R. Delvert.
**In back cover:** photos R. Delvert, B. and G. Delluc, A. Roussot, B. and G. Delluc, J. Plassart, B. and G. Delluc.

# Table of contents






Ce livre a été imprimé par Pollina à Luçon (85)
La photogravure est de Photogravure d'Aquitaine et Labogravure À Bordeaux (33)

ISBN : 978-2-81770-018-2
Éditeur : 29393.01.03.07.11
N° d'impression : L57532